Corgi Capers:

Curtain Calls and Fire Halls

Val Muller

ALL RIGHTS RESERVED

Publisher's Note:
This is a work of fiction. All names, characters, places, and events are the work of the author's imagination. Any resemblance to real persons, places, or events is coincidental.

Cover Art: **Val Muller**

ISBN 13: 978-0692322123
ISBN 10: 0692322124

www.dwbchildrensline.com

DWB PUBLISHING
Childrens Line

Dedication

To Eric,
for introducing me
to the fuzzy little gremlins.

From The Author:

My ultimate goal is to bring joy to readers through the pages of these books, and talking to readers makes this series come alive for me. Thank you to the readers of the *Corgi Capers* series so far—for the positive feedback, support, and reviews. A special thank-you to the Corgi Community, including Iron Corgi Maggie Thatcher (for her organizational leadership) and Denby Dog (for his inspiring strength and in whose memory this book is published)—a constant reminder to corgi strong!

A special thank you to the members of Corgi Nation and corgi fans who entered the Name That Cat contest, and an extra special "Arooo!" to the winners: Laura Flanagan (with Gavin Flanagan) and Wendy Walker, who each chose a name for a character in this book. Another "Arooo!" to Kat Savatinova, who generously won the auction to raise money for Denby Dog and chose to name a special character after this very special dog. I hope I have done justice to the inspiration that Denby provided—and continues to provide— every day, uniting two- and four-legged friends around the globe.

Thanks to Michelle Muller for the "hawk eyes" and to Eric Egger for his help in proofreading, editing, and shopping before snowstorms to give me time to write. Thanks to my sister Lisa for "reading when angry" and to Gavin McKay for his insightful feedback. Thank you to Kathryn Ives for answering my crazy questions about cats. To my parents, once again, for fostering years of creativity; I am privileged to be a "grown-up" who still sees magic in the world. Thanks to the creative and talented Voula Trip (www.VoulaTrip.com) for the headshot. And, of course, thanks to Marie McGaha, Bobbie Shafer, and Debbie Roppolo at DWB, for the support and encouragement.

And as always, a special thanks to Leia and Yoda for their quirky and inspirational personalities, constant companionship, and unconditional love.

~ One ~

With his notebook on his lap, Adam sat in the back of the minivan. He felt like Detective Riley Couth reviewing files before starting a new case. Fedora pulled down to one side, he opened to page one. In handwritten notes, it read:

Stoney Brook Volunteer Fire Company
New Volunteer Training
Wednesday, November 13
5 p.m.
Jeff Kurle, Fire Chief

Adam ran his hand over the letters and took a deep breath. Then he looked toward the house. Where was Mom? He couldn't be late on his first day. He leaned into the front seat and turned on the GPS. If Mom was going to be late, at least he could help speed things along.

"Welcome," the electronic voice said. "Input destination."

Adam typed in the address to the fire hall. He already knew it by heart: 100 Red Engine Drive, Stoney Brook, Pennsylvania. He had just pushed "calculate route" when a series of loud barks distracted him.

He hopped out of the car.

"Zeph? What is it?" His breath made ghostly mist in the cold November air as he hustled toward the barking.

"Zeph?"

Adam ran to the back of the house, where Courtney stood at the fence gate. He stood behind a bushy Rhododendron to observe the scene.

"Where is she?" Courtney screamed.

Mom walked the perimeter calling, "Sapphie? Sapphie!"

"I don't understand." Courtney crossed her arms. "The gate is locked. We filled the hole she dug. How does she keep escaping?"

"She'll come back, Courtney. This is the third time

she's escaped, and she came back the first two."

"The *fourth* time," Courtney said. "And the third time she was gone for hours." Courtney pouted her lips. "I want her back *now*."

"Maybe Zeph can find her," Adam said.

Courtney and Mom turned to him, startled. Adam stepped out from behind the bush the way Detective Riley Couth does when revealing himself to a suspect.

"Aroooo!" Zeph howled and wagged his stubbly tail.

Courtney crossed her arms. "Like Zeph will be able to do anything. That dog is afraid of his own shadow."

Zeph sat and cocked his head. Adam smiled at him. "Put him on a leash. I bet he can sniff out Sapphie's trail."

Courtney looked at Mom, who nodded.

"Can I, really?"

Adam nodded. "Just keep him on his leash. We don't need *two* corgis on the loose."

"Good idea," Mom said.

Courtney ran inside for Zeph's leash. Meanwhile, Mom looked down at the keys in her hand. "What was I supposed to do this afternoon?" she asked no one in particular. "I came out here with my jacket and my car keys. There was something I was supposed to do..."

Adam cleared his throat. Mom looked at him. "The firehouse," he said.

"Oh, I almost forgot! Today's training day for volunteers. We'd better get going." She jingled the car keys and hurried toward the driveway.

Adam bent down and stuck his hand through the slats of the picket fence. "You be a good boy, Zeph."

Zeph wiggled his stumpy tail and answered Adam with a loud "Aroooo!"

"Help find your sister," Adam said.

Zeph sat quietly.

"I'll be back later. Be good."

Adam gave Zeph a good scratch behind the ears and then ran off to join his mother in the car just as Courtney emerged from inside with Zeph's leash.

~ * ~

The fire hall looked deserted—much quieter than the last time Adam had been there for the Fourth of July crab feed. With baseball games, he'd been too busy to attend any of the other events. Now that baseball season was over, his parents suggested he should volunteer there, at least until baseball started again in the spring.

"I'll come back at six-thirty," Mom said. "Unless you want me to stay."

The parking lot was nearly empty. It looked like none of the other parents were staying, either. Adam shook his head. "I'll be okay by myself."

"I've got some grocery shopping to do, then. It's never too early to look for deals on ingredients for Thanksgiving dinner. I'm sure there's a supermarket on this side of town. I wonder if I turn right out of the parking lot, or left..."

"Just use your GPS," Adam reminded her. "Otherwise, you might get lost again and end up with two *more* corgis. Imagine how Dad would react with *four* corgis running around the house!" He laughed.

"I think we have enough animals for one family." Mom tapped the GPS screen. "She's alive and well. Now you have fun at the fire hall."

Adam looked around. "Too bad I don't know any of the other volunteers. It woulda been cool if Patrick coulda volunteered with me. But him and his father are crazy about baseball. He's training all winter."

Mom snickered. "*He* and his father. And it's would *have* and could *have*. A member of the Hollinger family should always use proper grammar." She nodded. "I'm sure you'll meet lots of great new friends."

"Okay, Mom. But remember, six-thirty. Don't get lost."

"I'll try not to." She looked at the fire hall. "Hey, look at that sign. There shouldn't be an apostrophe in

'CRAB'S,' and it's certainly not capitalized in the middle of a sentence like that, when none of the other words are capitalized..."

Adam rolled his eyes as he reached for his notebook. His new teacher had encouraged him to write down his experiences from his run-in with the burglar during the summer, and the habit stuck. Like his favorite comic book hero, he decided he would keep records of his new adventures.

He left his fedora, though. Hopefully there wouldn't be a mystery to solve on his first day of volunteering. He hopped out of the car and closed the door before Mom went on another rant about bad grammar. He heard her pull away as he walked up the gravel path leading to the twelve cement steps—the back door into the fire hall. At the top of the stairs, the sign read, "Volunteers Only."

"That's me," Adam said, tucking his notebook under his arm and taking a deep breath. "Here we go." Then he opened the door and stepped inside.

~ * ~

Courtney pulled Zeph down the street, wondering which way to go. In the past, Sapphie had run off in all directions. No telling where she went this time. Useless Zeph kept staring at Courtney, and each time she stopped he wagged his tail and howled.

"Zeph, stop looking at *me*. I can't tell you where to go. You need to take the lead. Use your nose. Find your sister. Find Sapphie."

Zeph's eyes sparkled. He sat at Courtney's feet and looked right at her. "Whoo! Arooooo!" His tail wagged.

"You're almost as useless as Adam. Come on, let's go this way." She pulled him toward the cul-de-sac. The cold November wind whispered through the bare trees, swirling a torrent of leaves on the street.

Zeph squealed.

"Oh, Zeph, they're only leaves. You can't be afraid of *everything*. Sniff around and find Sapphie."

13

Zeph continued down the street, sniffing once in a while.

"Sapphie!" Courtney called. "Where are you?"

But only the wind answered her.

Courtney paused at the end of the cul-de-sac, calling for Sapphie. The older Sapphie grew, the braver she became—and more disobedient, too. Courtney would have to tell the trainer about this new behavior during Friday's class. Courtney was supposed to be proving to her family how responsible she could be, but Sapphie was making that nearly impossible. It was hard to prove you had it all together when your dog kept running away.

"Sapphie, come over here!"

Zeph startled as a door opened at the house at the top of the hill. He barked at the familiar figure that emerged.

"Hi Cassie," Courtney called up.

"Aroooo!"

Cassie squinted down her driveway. "Courtney? Everything okay? I heard you shouting."

"Sapphie ran off again. Is she with you or Belle?"

Cassie hurried down the driveway. "No, not this time. Sorry. She stopped sneaking into my house after Halloween. Your mother told me you had started taking her to training classes. I assumed she stopped breaking loose."

"No. She still escapes." Courtney sighed. "I guess she found somewhere more interesting to sneak off to than your house."

Cassie forced a smile. "I'm sure she'll show up. She always does. If I see her, I'll call you right away."

"Call the house phone," Courtney said. "I'm still grounded from my cell except on weekends." Courtney looked down at her toes. "You know—because of what happened on Halloween."

Cassie nodded. "But you're turning over a new leaf, as they say. Your mom tells me you're volunteering at the retirement home."

"It's not volunteering if you're forced to do it," Courtney sighed. "But yes, I'm *volunteering* there."

"That reminds me." Cassie rubbed her lip. "I had a theatre-related topic to discuss with you. You can probably already tell my performance of *Macbeth* is over." Cassie spun around to show off her outfit—a long, flowing purple skirt and grey sweater.

"I assumed it was finished since you stopped wearing your cape—I mean, your *costume*—everywhere." Courtney laughed. "I enjoyed your performance, though. It was a fun play, even if it was Shakespeare. I don't know why he had to write in Old English."

Cassie laughed. "It's not Old English, silly. But I'm glad you liked the play. Anyway, I wanted to talk to you about something. My theatre company has a school outreach program."

"An outreach program?"

Cassie nodded. "The goal is to bring theatre to middle schools. I talked to the principal at your school, and I got permission to direct a play there. We'll be holding auditions next week, and we're scheduled to perform the play in early December. I thought you might like to audition."

Courtney blushed. "I guess I could. Mom and Dad would like me to be more involved at school. What's the play about?"

"It's a comedy called *Mister Baxter's Bookish Mess.* It takes place in a neighborhood bookstore, and all the neighbors end up stopping by—as customers—but things get all mixed up." Cassie laughed. "Anyway, there's even a part for a dog. I thought maybe, since you're training her now, Sapphie would be good for the role."

Courtney bit her lip. "Don't you think Zeph would be better for the role? I mean, he's much better behaved than Sapphie. He's afraid of practically everything, so he never does anything bad."

Courtney looked down at Zeph, who sat there

obediently. He was *too* good, if that was possible. Nothing like Sapphie.

Cassie bent down to pat Zeph on the head. "Maybe. But I believe in second chances. I think Sapphie can rise to the occasion if we give her another chance."

"Or maybe five other chances." Courtney sighed and turned around, hoping to spot her dog. But little Sapphie was nowhere in sight. Courtney turned back to Cassie.

"Don't worry, Courtney. We'll find her."

"Wish I was as sure as you." She shivered. "Anyway, about this play. How often would we rehearse? Early December seems soon."

"Mondays, Tuesdays, Wednesdays, and Thursdays after school. It's an intense program to get you ready to perform in just a few weeks."

"Sounds intense."

Cassie smiled. "I once wrote, learned, and performed a play in twenty-four hours. That was in college. This is a cake walk."

Courtney nodded. "Four days a week. That would leave my Fridays open for dog training. And my Saturdays for volunteering at the nursing home." She sighed. "Mom and Dad have my days pretty well-planned now."

Cassie smiled. "I look forward to seeing you next week at auditions, then."

"There's just one problem." Courtney spun around.

"What's that?"

"Your star canine is still missing." Courtney cupped her hands over her mouth. "Sapphie!" she called.

"Sapphie!" called Cassie.

"Aroooo!" Zeph howled. He faced away from the woods at the end of the cul-de-sac, and Courtney wasn't sure whether it was the cold or the darkening evening, but Zeph seemed to be shivering.

~ Two ~

Inside the fire hall, Adam took off his jacket, hanging it on a peg by the door. Three other coats hung there, too—two larger than his and one smaller. Above the coat pegs were two rows of shelves stacked with boxes. One box was labeled, "napkins—volunteers only." The other read, "plasticware."

Soft voices from inside the fire hall beckoned Adam, so he grasped his notebook and left the small coatroom. The expansive fire hall was empty except for a small table set up in the corner. Without any of the other tables, the room looked huge—bigger than the high school basketball auditoriums Adam had seen on his way to the locker room during All Star baseball season.

"Have a seat," a loud, deep voice called. A tall, blond-haired teenager motioned for Adam to sit at the table. Adam hurried over, stealing another glance at the teen. He looked at least as tall as Adam's mother, and he seemed to be snarling a little. With the teen's spiky hair, Adam couldn't help but think of JJ, Courtney's former friend, a tenth-grader who was always up to no good. Once in a while, Adam still had nightmares about JJ and the whole mess at Halloween, but keeping busy—doing things like volunteering or playing baseball—helped him to keep his mind on more pleasant things.

"You must be Adam," the teenager said. "You're the last of the three new volunteers to arrive. The first rule of volunteering is that you have to be on time."

Adam swallowed hard. "See, my mom gets distracted..." Adam stuttered. "And my sister's dog..."

But the teenager only shook his head. "Have a seat." Adam sat in the closest chair he could find. The teenager cleared his throat. "I'm Spencer. I've been volunteering here for six years already. I'm training to be a firefighter, and now that I'm sixteen, I get to ride along on fire calls if there's room. Chief Kurle recently put me in charge of managing the young volunteers, so if you have any questions, you ask me directly. Clear?"

"Yes," Adam answered in unison with the two other voices. He took a moment to glance to his right. In the middle of the table sat a boy who looked a year or two younger than Adam.

"I'm Gavin," said the curly, brown-haired boy. "Gavin Apuzzo. My brother's a firefighter in Texas, and I want to be like him someday."

"I'm Adam." He took a moment to scribble *Gavin Apuzzo* in his notebook. "I'm in fifth grade, and my parents thought it would be good for me to volunteer in the off-season."

Spencer's eyes narrowed. "Fires don't have an off-season," he said.

Adam nodded and waited for Spencer to break eye contact before writing *Spencer* in his notebook, followed by *no off-season.*

"I'm Spark," said the third person at the table. "My real name's Bianca." She wore her ebony hair in long braids, and the red Stoney Brook Firehouse jacket she wore glowed like a flame against her mahogany skin. She looked familiar, but Adam couldn't place her.

"I'm in seventh grade," she said. "My dad's a firefighter here. He's been teaching me about fire safety all my life, and after what happened last year, he thought I should start volunteering." She smiled proudly.

"What happened last year?" asked Gavin.

"I was at a rehearsal for my middle school's chorus concert, and I smelled something burning. Everyone else ignored it. Even the teacher thought it was just someone burning food in the cafeteria. But I insisted." She crossed her arms and smiled. "I asked for a bathroom pass, but I snuck backstage instead. I saw a bunch of wires coming out from the wall and into the lighting control box. I smelled the smoke coming from that direction. I told the teacher right away. We had to evacuate the school, and when the firemen arrived, they said the wires were old and had overheated inside the walls. If I hadn't insisted, they might have actually caught on fire. They ran a whole story about it in the newspaper." She smiled. "My picture was on the front page."

"That's where I recognize you from!" Adam said. "I read that article. My teacher has a bulletin board where she puts articles about local heroes. The headline was *The Girl Who Saved Her School*. Bianca Harper."

Spark smiled. "That's me."

"My teacher read that article to the whole class, and it's still up there on the bulletin board." He neglected to mention that it was right next to the article about him when he was recognized for helping to catch the serial burglar in his neighborhood.

"Wow, that's cool," Spark said. "What school?"

"Stoney Brook Elementary."

"Oh," she said. "I live on the other side of town. I went to Shepherd Meadow Elementary, which feeds into Cold Spring Middle School."

"I go to Shepherd Meadow Elementary, too," said Gavin.

Adam nodded, writing down *Shepherd Meadow Elementary* and *Cold Spring Middle School* in his notebook. Then he added, *Spark Harper—VERY confident.*

"See that picture?" Spark pointed to a framed picture along the wall. "See that guy in the second row holding the end of the fire hose?"

"Yeah?" asked Adam.

"Well that's my dad. He's a firefighter here, and I'm so proud of him." She smiled.

Adam squinted at the picture. He recognized the same determined brow on Spark and her father. He looked at the other pictures along the wall. They went back several decades—all the way to the 1970s, when the fire company was established, and they displayed laminated pictures of volunteer firemen from past and present. Above the pictures was a framed, enlarged image of a postage stamp commemorating the firefighters who served and died on September 11, 2001. Adam remembered learning about that date in school. He couldn't imagine being a firefighter running toward, or even into, a burning building.

Bravery, he scribbled into his notebook.

"Okay, enough chit-chat." Spencer clapped his hands. "We've got less than half an hour to go through the rules before the others arrive."

"The others?" asked Gavin.

"The other volunteers. They're arriving around six to set up for the wedding."

"Wedding?" Spark's eyes glowed.

Adam and Gavin exchanged nervous glances.

"There's a wedding reception being held here Friday night. Since we're not using the fire hall tonight or Thursday, we're going to set up for the reception tonight. It'll be your first assignment as volunteers."

The three nodded.

"Now let's take a quick tour." Spencer motioned, and the three volunteers stood to follow him. "This here's the kitchen." He pointed to the room behind their table. "Only adults are allowed to cook in the kitchen, but you three can do stuff like lug bags of ice in the pantry. If they're not too heavy," he said to Adam and Gavin.

He slid a rolling metal divider up, revealing a darkened kitchen with a huge metal counter and a stove top larger than Adam's kitchen table. "This window here opens to the kitchen and allows food to be passed through. Again, only grownups can handle food and serve it, but you kids can collect people's meal tickets and pass out plasticware and napkins and stuff." Spencer slammed down the rolling metal divider. Then he turned and walked to the middle of the hall. "During events, we put trash cans there, there, there, and there. In the four corners. You three can empty the trash bags when they get full. Bring them to the dumpster out back, and put a new trash bag in the can. Same for the trash cans in the bathrooms."

The three of them scrunched up their noses, but they tried not to let Spencer see.

"Mostly we need help before and after the events, setting up all the tables and chairs, then cleaning them and storing them again." Spencer looked around. "Now the older kids who are trusted get to sell candy bars after dinner. There's also a fifty-fifty raffle. Adults are supposed to sell those tickets, but Chief told me he might let me help out next time." Spencer's face grew serious. "But none of you newbies are allowed to touch any of the money. It's for the firehouse, and it's important none of it goes missing again."

Adam jotted down *No money can go missing* in his notebook. Then he narrowed his eyes and wrote, *Again.*

Gavin's eyes grew wide. "Why? How much money is there usually?"

"The raffle usually goes up to about five hundred dollars. Half goes to the winner, and half to the firehouse. It's not pocket change, got it?"

Gavin nodded. "Imagine what we could buy with five hundred dollars," he whispered to Adam.

Adam smiled, thinking about all the comic books, baseball gear, and dog toys that money could buy. He wrote *$500* in his notebook.

Spencer squinted. "Don't get any ideas."

Adam's scalp tingled. It seemed there might be a mystery after all. He wished he had worn his fedora.

"Alright, let's go out to the garage," Spencer said. "I'll show you where the dumpsters are, and then Fire Chief Kurle wants to meet you and show you Engine Ten. If you have questions, ask 'em while we walk."

Spark pushed to the front of the group. "I have a question. Are there many other girls who volunteer, or is it mostly guys?"

Spencer answered without slowing his brisk pace. "There are plenty of girls who volunteer. We don't have any female firefighters—the test is really hard for girls to pass wearing all that gear, but we've got plenty of women involved with the firehouse."

"Hard to pass?" She narrowed her eyes. "What? Why?"

"Just because guys and girls are built differently," Spencer said. He held up his hands. "No offense."

Spark clicked her teeth. "No offense taken, Spencer, but I'm not one to be taken lightly. Tell me, do you know why my nickname is 'Spark'?"

"No." Spencer opened the back door, leading them outside.

"They call me 'Spark' because once I get a spark of an idea, I won't let go 'til I see it through."

Spencer shrugged. "Here are the dumpsters. When you empty the trash, it goes in here. The blue one is for recycling. Members of the community are allowed to bring their recycling here, too. If it gets too full, let the firefighters know."

Spark huffed. "Tell me, Spencer. This really difficult test—have *you* passed it?"

"No."

"Hmph! Guess *you* aren't so tough, then."

"I'm training for it." Spencer crossed his arms. "No one is allowed to take the test until they turn eighteen. The test involves going into a live fire. Very dangerous."

Adam turned to Gavin, his eyes wide.

Spark snickered. "I'm not afraid. I have over four years to get ready for the test, and then I can be a firefighter just like my dad."

Spencer sighed and opened the door to the huge garage housing Engine Ten, the bright red fire truck owned by the Stoney Brook Fire Company.

"Wow!" Adam said.

"Cool!" agreed Gavin.

Spark sighed like she was bored. "I've seen it many

times," she explained. "I even rode it."

A man with a clipboard stepped out from behind the engine. He was tall and muscular with a bit of a belly, and he wore a long, graying beard. His jolly mannerisms reminded Adam of a combination of Santa Claus and Coach Harris.

"These must be the three new recruits," he chuckled. "Spark, I already know you. The young one must be Gavin Apuzzo, and of course I've read all about Adam Hollinger in the paper."

Gavin and Spark turned to Adam, but Adam just kept his head low and hoped his ears didn't get too red.

"I'm Fire Chief Kurle. Everyone either calls me Kurle—like curly hair—or Chief. My number one rule is—"

"To be on time," Adam said, looking at Spencer.

"No, not exactly," Kurle said.

Spencer averted his eyes.

"Being on time is important, but keeping each other safe is the most important thing." He pointed to the fire engine. "The men who ride the apparatus all have families. People like Spark's father. We need to keep them safe. The money we raise through our events and fundraisers helps keep our equipment in good shape, and that saves lives. This is a completely volunteer operation. We depend on our fundraisers and volunteers like the three of you to make firefighting possible."

He looked down at the three young volunteers, smiling. "Now who wants a tour of the engine?"

Adam stared up at the front of the truck. It looked quite intimidating with its huge front windows. On the roof were a series of red and white lights. On the bumper, Adam could see two horns—he could guess how loud they might be—and a speaker for the siren.

Kurle motioned for them to follow him. They started at the back of the truck. "This, my friends, is Engine Company Ten." He patted the back of the engine the way he would pat a good friend on the back.

23

Adam looked up at the tall truck and noticed a sign that said, "Engine: keep back 500 feet."

"Now this here," Kurle said, pointing to a series of dials on the side of the truck, "is a pump panel."

"Looks complicated." Adam squinted. The dials looked like a series of eyes, with levers like eyebrows, all staring at him.

"It is. Our drivers are carefully trained. When they arrive at a fire, the driver will hurry over to this pump panel. These dials let him know how much water is getting to the firefighters." He pointed to a large round nozzle. "This is where we can hook up to a fire hydrant when one is available."

Spark raised her hand. "What if there isn't a fire hydrant available?"

Kurle nodded. "Good question. We have backup trucks called tankers that provide water. Some are from Stoney Brook, but others are from nearby locations. We all help each other in the case of a true emergency."

He pulled out a hose. "Notice how our hoses are flat. They're not attached to anything right now. Firefighters hook up the hoses when they're needed." He held out the hose for everyone to touch. "They're flat now, but they expand when filled up with water." Kurle made a muscle. "All the equipment is heavy. The hoses, too. Takes a great deal of training to become a firefighter."

Spark crossed her arms and narrowed her eyes.

"Then we have all kinds of other important tools." Kurle slid out a drawer. "Ever heard of the *Jaws of Life*?"

Gavin raised his hand. "They can cut through car doors when people are trapped."

"That's right. They can cut through car rooftops or break open doors. If you're ever stuck in a car after an accident, these are your best friends." He lifted the instrument out of the drawer. It was huge—like a pair of pliers made for a giant. Adam watched the muscles in Kurle's forearm as he lifted the tool and realized how heavy it was.

"Let me try." Spark held out her hands. Kurle lowered the tool gently into her arms, though he didn't let go completely. At first Spark's arms nearly collapsed with the weight of them. But she clenched her jaw and lifted.

Kurle smiled down at her. "You remind me of your father." He replaced the Jaws of Life into the drawer and continued the tour. "There are other little nooks and crannies. Here's a door on the side of the truck." He opened it, revealing three fire extinguishers. "Just in case. We've got some fire extinguishers and an extra helmet and air pack."

"Air pack?" Gavin asked.

"During a fire, the air becomes unbreathable. In fact, during house fires, pets often die because they can't get enough air—rather than being harmed in the fire itself. That's why they tell you to get down on the ground during a fire. Get on the ground and crawl to safety. The air lowest to the ground is safest to breathe. The bad air will rise to the ceiling."

Adam shivered, picturing what might happen if Zeph and Sapphie got trapped in a fire.

Spark nodded. "I've known that since kindergarten."

"Come on, let's take a look inside." They followed Kurle through a door in the side. "There's the driver's seat."

Adam noticed there was no passenger seat up front. Instead, where the front passenger would normally sit, there was a radio and all sorts of other equipment. The steering wheel was huge—nothing like the steering wheels in his parents' cars.

Kurle continued. "From here, the driver can control the horn, the lights, and the siren. Go on outside, and I'll show you what it looks like."

The three volunteers climbed out and watched as Kurle cycled through all the light combinations. There was flashing red and alternating white.

"Want to hear the siren?" he asked.

"Yes!" cried Adam and Gavin.

"No!" cried Spark. "We'll go deaf."

Kurle laughed. "She's probably right, boys. To turn on the siren in this closed garage would be a little loud. When the weather gets nicer, and we have a volunteer day, I'll show you all that stuff—outdoors."

He motioned them inside. "Come back in. I'll show you where the passengers sit." Inside hung three oxygen tanks, and several flashlights were attached to the walls. "We also keep medical equipment on board. We're trained to deal with medical emergencies if we arrive on a scene first. There are also axes, hooks..." he pointed to the roof. "The ladder up there, of course..."

Adam followed Kurle outside and stared at the red and chrome engine. He looked at Gavin and couldn't help but share the excitement that reflected on Gavin's face. He'd never thought about becoming a firefighter before, and though he wasn't sure it was the right job for him, he was glad to be involved and promised himself he'd help the fire company as long as he lived in Stoney Brook.

Kurle patted Adam and Gavin on the back. "Okay, boys. Spark. Fun's over. Now the work begins. Have you boys ever decorated for a wedding reception before?"

The boys shook their heads. Their smiles faded. Spark smirked.

"First time for everything, boys. Now hop to it."

~ Three ~

Zeph plopped onto his rocketship bed and sniffed the cushion. Ah, the unmistakable scent of Sapphie! She smelled like energy and adventure and dirt and bugs and Maximillion's Pretty Puppy Shampoo. Zeph couldn't help but whine. He missed his sister, and he was getting worried. She'd been disappearing more lately, and with the weather changing, what if she got lost in the cold?

Why couldn't she stay inside the fence like a good dog?

"Zeph, be quiet, okay?" Courtney pleaded. She was seated at the computer, but she wasn't giggling like she normally did. She seemed serious and sad, and her foot kept twitching. "I'm trying to find her, okay? And I can't concentrate if all I hear is you whining."

Zeph squeaked once more and lowered his head onto his bed, the one his sister always stole from him and slept in. Why couldn't she be here to steal it from him now?

Courtney squinted at the computer screen and picked up the phone. Normally when she used the phone, she was sneaky and giggly, and Adam didn't like it one bit— and that meant Zeph didn't, either. Normally when Courtney used the phone, Zeph and Adam would leave the room before too long. But Adam was away, and Courtney wasn't giggling. Something was wrong.

"Hello, Mrs. Stoy. It's Courtney Hollinger." Courtney was speaking into the phone in a hushed voice. She sounded almost as kind as Adam. "I'm sorry to disturb you. Oh, I didn't realize you were getting ready for bed so early." She paused. "Yes, ma'am. I know it gets dark early this time of year...No, ma'am...No, ma'am...I was looking for my dog. If you see her, would you please give me a call?" She paused again. "No, ma'am, I don't expect you would be going out anymore tonight. No, ma'am. Thank you. Good night."

Courtney slammed down the phone and screeched, and Zeph jolted upright, scampering across the floor. He stopped at the sliding glass door, hoping he'd see Sapphie sitting there waiting. But he knew she wouldn't be. Sapphie had all kinds of ways of jumping over the fence to get out of the back yard, but she wasn't very good at getting back in. On the outside, the fence was too smooth to offer any footholds. If Sapphie came back—*when* she came back, Zeph reminded himself—she'd come to the front door.

Zeph cried and hurried to the front door. He sniffed at the draught coming from underneath. It even smelled like frost. He sat on the chilly tile of the entryway and listened for sounds of his sister. The cold crept along his fur and skin, and he shivered. He could only imagine how frozen Sapphie would be outdoors.

Zeph turned back to Courtney, who was on the phone again. "Thank you, Mrs. Davenport," Courtney was saying. "I'm sure she'll come home soon, too. I'm just so worried."

Zeph was worried, too. And despite the cold, he resolved to wait right there on the tile near the front door until his sister came home.

~ * ~

When Adam, Gavin, and Spark returned from the tour, the fire hall was already full of noise and volunteers. A dozen long tables were arranged in the room with open space in the middle. Two women waddled down the center of the room, struggling to carry a white archway. They wore pearl earrings and high heels. Their shoes didn't look very comfortable for doing physical work.

"Stay out of their way," a volunteer whispered to Adam. "One's the mother of the bride. The other's the mother of the groom. They want the wedding to be perfect, and their nerves are strung tight."

"Thanks," Adam said, studying the volunteer. She looked a year or two older than Adam, though with girls it was hard to tell. Her wavy hair hung to her shoulders, and her frazzled hair and t-shirt reminded Adam how hard he'd have to work as a volunteer here.

"I'm Emily," she said. "Grab an end." She held out a flowing purple tablecloth. "We have to cover all the tables in purple."

Adam placed his notebook under the table and grabbed an end. "I'm Adam."

"I know." Emily lifted the cloth over the table and Adam helped smooth it out. "My dad's a firefighter here. I have to volunteer whether I like to or not, so I hear all the gossip. Stick with me if you want to learn the ropes."

Adam smiled up at her, but she didn't smile back. He turned toward Gavin, but he and Spark were already on the other side of the room tying colored ribbons on all the folding chairs.

Adam turned back to Emily. "So you don't like volunteering here?"

"I didn't say that. It's okay and everything. It's just that my parents never gave me a choice. They planned for me to be volunteering here before I was even born."

"Oh."

Emily took another tablecloth from the box and moved to a second table. Feeling a little like Riley Couth beginning an investigation, Adam wondered if he should ask Emily about the missing money that Spencer mentioned earlier. But Emily kept talking.

"So my dad told me all about you and Gavin and Spark, too. I know you're the kid who helped stop that burglar this summer."

Adam lowered his head so Emily wouldn't see his burning ears.

"I don't know much about Gavin. Just that he goes to Shepherd Meadow Elementary. And Spark—well, everyone around here knows about Spark. My dad wishes I'd be more like her, but I can't help it. It seems like firefighting is transferred through the blood, and it must have skipped over my generation in the family."

"Sorry." Adam frowned and smoothed out the second tablecloth.

"It's okay." Emily sighed. "I only have to volunteer until I turn sixteen. Then I'll be allowed to get a job somewhere. Just like Bill."

"Bill?"

"William Blazier." Emily pointed to a boy in the corner. "Everyone calls him Bill. Firefighting runs in his family, too. His dad got injured real bad in a fire a couple years ago. Blazing debris fell on him during a collapse. Severed some nerves in his leg."

Adam cringed.

Emily handed him another tablecloth. "He can't walk so good anymore. Had to give up firefighting, obviously. Hobbles around with a cane and always in pain. He still volunteers, though. Comes here to make crab chowder for crab feed nights. He and his wife are still making Bill volunteer, though. They want him to be a firefighter one day. He won't, though."

"How do you know?"

"Bill's terrified of fires now—ever since what happened to his father. He won't tell his parents, though. In fact, he doesn't like to talk about it at all, but he and I have discussed it before. I know he's terrified. He's going to quit the minute he turns sixteen. His parents won't stop him, either."

"Why not?"

Emily clicked her teeth. "He's going to get a job when he turns sixteen, and with his dad's injury, his family doesn't have much money. They could use an extra paycheck. They won't stop him."

Adam nodded, taking another peek at Bill. He couldn't imagine what it would be like to have an injured parent, or to be worried about money. As he turned back to help Emily, he realized how fortunate he really was. He couldn't wait to pick up his notebook again and jot down all he had learned.

~ * ~

Courtney finished with the telephone, and Zeph kept an eye on her from the frozen entryway. She was sniffling, and drops of water ran down her cheeks. He felt like he should help, but he never saw such a thing happen to Adam. He wasn't sure what to do. It was clear none of the neighbors had seen Sapphie. Maybe drops of water fell down people's cheeks when they were very worried. Zeph was worried, too. He whined as Courtney pulled on her boots.

"C'mon, Zeph. We're going back out to look for Sapphie." Zeph sat still while Courtney clipped on his leash. Then he sprung toward the sliding glass door and Zeph hurried into the backyard, pulling Courtney behind him. His nose twitched, and he lunged at the fence, turning toward the woods beyond the cul-de-sac. He smelled Sapphie on the wind.

"Arooo!"

"Hold on," Courtney said. "It's too dark. I need a flashlight." She dropped the leash to go inside, and Zeph clawed at the fence.

"Whooo!" he howled.

A pair of sneaky eyes emerged in the darkness, and Zeph skittered away.

The eyes went dark for a moment before a familiar voice broke the silence. "Fraidy, fraidy, *fraidy*! It's me, Zeph."

"Arooo!" shouted Zeph. "Sapphie! Sapphie! *Sapphie!*"

"Help me get back in," Sapphie demanded.

"Your Courtney's coming out. She'll help you."

"Thanks for not tattling on me, Zeph. I saw you walking with Courtney. I know you saw me."

"I didn't see you. I smelled you in the wo-wo-woods."

"Those woods are fun, fun, *fun*! And I've got a special secret in there."

31

"What kind of secret?"

"You'd probably be afraid of it. I better not say."

"You can't keep secrets from me, Sapphie." Zeph sat tall, puffing out his chest, trying to look brave.

"Of course I can." Sapphie spun around as if showing off.

Zeph stuck his nose through the fence. "But I'm your brother."

"If you want to know my secret, then come into the woods with me next time."

"The wo-wo—what? What do you mean, *next time*? You mean you're going back to the wo-wo-woods? When?"

"I dunno. Whenever I feel like it."

"Sapphie, you can't keep escaping like this."

"Why not? It's fun, fun, *fun*! You wouldn't believe all the fun smells in the woods. There was even something sticky and black. I rolled in it. See?" She spun around, showing off a dark stain on the white fairy saddle marking of her neck.

"I can smell that from here. Courtney won't be happy."

Sapphie cheered. "Sure she will."

"No. She's been so worried and even had water dropping from her eyes."

Sapphie licked her lips.

"Not water to drink. Water because she was worried."

Sapphie snarled. "Serves her right for taking me to those stupid classes every week."

"Those classes are to help you."

"I don't need help. I'm a princess. Princess Sapphie. That means—"

"Sapphie, you're supposed to be learning how to be a good dog." Zeph put his paw up on the fence. "Besides, what are you doing in the woods over there? I—"

Both dogs turned to the sound of the glass door opening. Sapphie barked, and Courtney, just emerging with her flashlight, squealed.

"Sapphie?"

She hurried past Zeph to open the gate, and Sapphie took a running leap into her arms.

"Oh, Sapphie, you smell horrible." She held Sapphie tight. "But I'd rather give you a bath than search for you in the dark."

Courtney kept talking, but Zeph wasn't paying too much attention to that. From the looks of it, neither was Sapphie. Both dogs were more worried at something Courtney had said, something that made them tremble— Courtney's mention of the feared, the dreaded, the terrible—

B-b-b-bath!

~ Four ~

When Adam came down for breakfast, Courtney was seated on the floor with Sapphie curled up on her lap.

"Are you eating out of a dog dish today?" he asked his sister, laughing.

Dad sat at the table, reading something on a tablet, and Mom was finishing making school lunches.

"No, Adam. I already ate. I'm just glad Sapphie's back. For your information, while you were busy at the fire house yesterday, she was loose for hours in the cold. Zeph was no help finding her, by the way."

Adam glanced at Zeph, who put his head down and darted back his ears. Adam shrugged, petting Zeph. "That's weird. Zeph should have been able to pick up her scent. He should have found her right away. Remember that time she was hiding in the basement? He found her then. And when she got stuck under all those newspapers...I wonder why he didn't this time."

"Maybe your dog isn't as special as you think he is."

Adam glared again at Courtney. "Anyhow, Sapphie seems glad to be back. She looks like a cat, all curled up there on your lap. I swear I can almost hear her purring."

"She's just snoring."

Dad looked up from his reading. "Courtney, you be sure to mention Sapphie's escapes at training class tomorrow. See what the instructor says. If she keeps escaping, we'll have to keep her inside when you aren't around to watch her."

"Oh, that reminds me," Courtney said. "I was talking to Cassie yesterday when I was looking for Sapphie. Cassie's doing this play. It's, like, a program with the middle schools. The play is called... well, I forget what it's called, but it's a comedy, and there's a part I can play and a part for a dog, and I thought that maybe me and Sapphie could—"

Mom cleared her throat from behind her coffee cup. "Sapphie and I," she corrected.

"Sapphie and *I*," Courtney continued. "We could be in it. It's Mondays through Thursdays after school for like a month."

"Courtney, try not to say 'like' so much."

"Yes, Mom." Courtney sighed. Then she looked up again. "You'd have to drop Sapphie off for rehearsals…and then you'd have to pick me up after we finished."

Mom raised an eyebrow. "Four days a week?"

Courtney snickered. "You let Adam go to baseball practice all the time."

"It would be good for her to be more involved," Dad said.

"I really liked the play we saw with them. *Macbeth*." Courtney smiled at Mom and made her eyes all big and watery. She was really good at that. Adam cringed.

Mom's eyes sparkled. "And I'm sure Cassie would be willing to drive you and Sapphie home after each rehearsal. I think it's a great idea."

Adam poured a bowl of cereal and slipped a morsel to Zeph under the table. "Sapphie acting?" Adam told Zeph. "Now this I've got to see."

~ * ~

Sapphie paced in the back of the minivan. Then she jumped from the seat to the floor and back again. Person Mom was looking in that shiny reflecty thing and muttering something to Courtney. It sounded like disapproval.

"Fine, Mom," Courtney said. Then she huffed. "Sometimes I hate Fridays." She turned to the back seat. "Sapphie, sit."

Sapphie shot to attention, wagging her stub of a tail. Courtney narrowed her eyes. That was something people only did when they were mad, and Sapphie certainly wasn't doing anything to make her mad. How dare she squint her eyes at a princess!

Sapphie jumped onto the floor and barked.

"Sapphie, quiet," Courtney ordered.

Sapphie sat and barked again. What was Courtney's problem? Didn't she understand that Sapphie was in a car, car, *car*? There was hardly anything more exciting than riding in a car—except toys and fetch and eating and—

Courtney reached back to grab Sapphie, but that silly Person Girl was too slow. Sapphie dashed under the seat and scurried to the back of the minivan. She ran to the corner and sniffed at the area where Zeph had an accident during the summer. She barked just thinking about how funny it was. A siren had been going by, and Zeph got so scared that he—

Sapphie stopped barking and cried. Where *was* Zeph? Why wasn't he here?

"Sapphie, quiet," Courtney said.

But Sapphie wouldn't be quiet until she saw her brother again. She wanted him now, now, *now*! Why couldn't she see him? She wanted to bite on his ear.

"Oh, Sapphie, *please* stop barking," Courtney whined. "We haven't even started our training class yet, and you're already being bad."

Before Sapphie could bark in protest, the car came to a stop, and Sapphie dashed to the door, bounding up and down. Maybe Zeph was there waiting.

Courtney sighed. "She looks like a baby kang-arooo," she told Person Mom. Sapphie reminded herself to ask Zeph what a "kang-arooo" was. She hoped it was a type of princess.

"Arooo!" Sapphie howled.

Courtney giggled. "Now you sound like Zeph."

The sound of her brother's name got Sapphie all excited again, and she clawed at the minivan's door.

"The instructor says we're supposed to keep them calm before class, and I thought she was calm after her walk this afternoon, but now she's wild again. I think keeping Sapphie calm is impossible."

Courtney jangled the leash and reached back to clip

it to Sapphie's collar, but Sapphie would have none of that. She squealed and leapt into Courtney's arms. If that Person Girl insisted on taking her away from Zeph, then the least she could do was carry her across the parking lot. Sapphie looked around, twitching her nose at all the cars parked there.

She squealed at the familiar scent coming from the building. No, no, *no*! It was that class again! She had been there a few times already, and each time, Zeph hadn't been with her. She asked Zeph what a "class" was, but he just kept telling her it was where she would learn to be a good girl.

"Being good is boring," Sapphie had told Zeph.

"It's boring, boring, *boring*!" Sapphie barked and barked, but Courtney didn't seem to be listening. Zeph was the only one who ever listened to Sapphie. She wished he was there with her. She wanted him now, now, *now*!

But she didn't have much time to wish. Soon, Courtney carried her to the door to the building and pushed it open. A wave of smells hit Sapphie, and her entire body stiffened, her nose twitching faster than ever. She smelled big dogs and little dogs, young dogs and old dogs, accidents and treats, toys and people. Her legs started running even though Courtney still held her in her arms.

"Put me down, down, *down*!" Sapphie howled.

"Stop barking, Sapphie!" Courtney said. "And hold still. Your claws are digging up my arms."

Sapphie was so close to jumping down when Sir appeared. He held out his hand to Person Mom. "Welcome back," he said in a deep, firm voice.

Sapphie quieted immediately, her ears darting back.

"I see little Sapphie is as wild as ever. Did you get her some exercise before coming today?"

Person Mom nodded. "Courtney did."

"I walked her, Sir," Courtney said, "but she still seems full of energy." Courtney placed Sapphie on the floor. Sapphie sat, eyes locked on Sir.

Sir rubbed his chin. Zeph said people did that when they were thinking. Sapphie didn't like thinking. It was too boring. Speaking of boring, Sir was the most boring person ever. He was even more boring than Adam or Zeph. He didn't like to do anything fun, and he didn't like to let anyone else do anything fun, either.

Sir kept his hand up. "Sapphie, stay." Sapphie kept her eyes locked on him. "Good girl." Sir was a sneaky one, and Sapphie wouldn't let him trick her. She sat still and listened carefully to the entire conversation. She had to watch what Sir might say to her Courtney.

"How has the training been going?"

Courtney shifted a little, wiggling the leash. "Okay, I guess."

"Just okay?"

"Yeah."

Person Mom cleared her throat. "Court, tell him."

Sir turned to Courtney. "What's been happening?"

Courtney looked down at Sapphie. Sapphie wagged her tail, but Courtney did not smile. Sapphie barked and jumped up, scratching at Courtney's knees.

Sir turned to her quickly and held up his hand. He was too sneaky. "Sit. Quiet. Stay." Sapphie immediately quieted and sat. She didn't like Sir. How did he always manage to trick her into listening? He always made her do things that were no fun.

"Sapphie's been sneaking off." Courtney looked down at her feet. She kept talking, but Sapphie lost interest. She already knew all the boring things Courtney was going to say about Sapphie sneaking into the woods. Who cares? So boring!

Instead, Sapphie sat still and listened to the echoes around her, her nose twitching all the while. In the middle of the room, behind a few shelves of Things Good to Eat, was the place with lots of dogs. She remembered from last time.

"Running away is very serious," Sir was saying. "It

could lead to…"

Boring, boring, *boring*! Sapphie needed to get to the other dogs. She tried jumping, but Sir gave her a sneaky look. She plopped back down, and when Courtney started talking again, Sapphie lowered herself to the ground completely. She crawled slowly toward the smell of dogs.

She peeked back at her people.

"…tie her with a rope," Person Mom was saying. "Or keep her indoors…"

Sir said something else that sounded just as boring, so Sapphie continued to crawl toward the smell of dogs. She could hear them, too. Many were panting. A few were barking, and one was even squealing. None of them quite sounded like her Shadow, though. Still, she kept crawling, crawling, until—

She forgot that Courtney had put her on a leash. She hadn't figured out how to escape those yet, and the leash pulled tight.

"Oh, Sapphie," Courtney sighed.

Sir snapped to attention. "Don't whine, Courtney. Simply do this." He held up his hand. "Sapphie, sit."

Sapphie immediately snapped to attention and scurried over, sitting at his feet.

Tricky.

"Good." Sir turned to Courtney. "See, you have to be firm with her. Not mean, but firm. Calm. Confident."

Sir kept talking, but Sapphie stopped listening. She needed to get to those other dogs, but she knew Sir would never let her. Only Courtney would. The nerve of Sir! With so many sounds and smells, the last thing Sapphie wanted to do was sit around. And if she couldn't play with the other dogs, then at least she should be able to run off into the woods to play with Shadow.

"Hmph!" she sighed.

"Alright," Person Mom said. "I'll be sitting in the back this time. Remember, Courtney, she's your dog. You need to establish control."

Sir walked away, heading toward the smell of other dogs, and Person Mom followed. Now was her chance! Sapphie jumped up and pulled toward the other dogs. Like a good Person, Courtney followed.

Sapphie barked to congratulate herself. Training Courtney was *so* easy. She'd have to tell Zeph.

~ * ~

Adam sat at home enjoying quiet time after a full week at school. Dad was out in his office working on some blueprints, Courtney was at obedience class with Sapphie and Mom, and Zeph was curled up at Adam's feet. For once, he had the family room all to himself. He held the latest issue of *Riley Couth, Super Sleuth* in front of him.

"Zeph, want to read this comic book with me?"

Zeph wagged his tail and barked.

Adam plopped onto the floor. Zeph leapt into his lap. "Mom and Courtney are coming back with pizza soon," he told Zeph. "We can read until then."

Zeph barked and snuggled in.

Adam cleared his throat and read the first page aloud. "Things had been quiet for Riley Couth lately. Too quiet. He could tell something was brewing in the city, and it was only a matter of time before trouble would break free again."

Adam turned to Zeph. "What do you think, boy?"

Zeph cocked his head.

"Do you think things here are too quiet? Do you think trouble's brewing somewhere? Or are things just going real well for a change?"

"Whooo," Zeph answered softly.

Adam scratched Zeph's ears and then turned back to his comic book. "It was a quiet, dark night. Riley was on his way home from a—"

The phone rang.

"Dad?" Adam called. But Dad was still in his office in the detached garage outside. "I'll get it, then." Adam shifted. "Sorry, Zeph. Gotta get up." Zeph skittered away as Adam grabbed the phone from the desk near the computer."

"Hello?"

"Hi, Adam. What's up?" said the voice on the other line.

"Patrick?"

"No, it's me, Gavin."

"Oh, hi, Gavin. What's up?"

"Just thought I'd call to talk about the fire house. I got your number from the list of volunteers Chief gave us. What do you think of volunteering so far?"

Adam shrugged. "It's not bad. Setting up for the wedding was easy. Well, except for those two mothers. What were their names?" Adam reached for his notebook.

"Mrs. Simmons and Mrs. Shoemaker," Gavin said.

Adam checked his notebook. "Good memory. Riley Couth would be proud."

"Riley *who*?" Gavin asked.

"Riley Couth. He's a detective in my comic book. He's always working on his memory, but he usually has to write stuff down. Like me."

"I'm really good at remembering stuff," said Gavin. "I'll never forget Mrs. Simmons or Mrs. Shoemaker."

Adam added a comment next to their names in his notebook: *Mrs. Simmons and Mrs. Shoemaker—picky wedding.* "Did you see the way they inspected those purple tablecloths?"

"Yes! They wanted to make sure there weren't any wrinkles at all. We had to re-do that one table three times."

"I know! It wasn't our fault that the tablecloth got all staticky." Adam looked at the clock. "I wonder how the reception's going. It should be starting right about now."

"I'm sure Bill and Emily will tell us all about it. Just glad we didn't have to be at the wedding!"

Adam snickered. "Mrs. Shoemaker and Mrs. Simmons would be furious if they saw two elementary kids at the wedding. But I heard Spark would be volunteering."

"She's different." Gavin hummed.

"She's motivated, alright."

"Are you volunteering tomorrow?" Gavin asked.

"Yep. They asked me if I'd rather clean up from the wedding reception in the morning or help run the spaghetti dinner in the evening. It fits better with my parents' schedules for them to drop me off for the dinner."

"That's when I'm volunteering, too," Gavin said. "I'm glad. Nice having someone my own age who's also new."

Gavin sounded a little nervous about the dinner, and Adam sighed with relief. Adam wasn't the only one!

"What do you think they'll have us do?" Adam asked.

"I'm not sure. Probably collect tickets, pass out forks and butter packets, and empty the trash."

"Doesn't sound too hard."

"I can't wait until I'm older." Gavin sighed dreamily.

"Why?"

"I think it would be exciting to be allowed to sell candy bars. Or help with the fifty-fifty raffle. Can you imagine being in charge of all that money?"

"It would be interesting." Adam scribbled in his notebook: *Gavin—money*. "I think Spencer said you have to be eighteen to sell raffle tickets, though. Older kids just get to help."

Gavin continued speaking. "Still, I think it would be exciting to have that much responsibility. My mom never lets me pay for anything on my own. Even if it's my allowance money, she takes it from me and gives it to the cashier. I just can't wait 'til I'm old enough to handle money by myself, you know?"

Adam smiled. "I remember when we first got the corgis. That night, my mom gave me money and let me go into the store myself and pay for everything, too, while she waited in the car."

Gavin sighed. "Must have been fun."

"It was."

Adam reached for his detective hat. "I just remembered something."

"What's that?"

"Remember what Spencer said? The money can't go missing *again*. Like maybe it happened already."

"You mean like somebody stole it?"

"Maybe." Adam let his mind drift. How would Riley Couth solve this mystery? Being new to the fire hall, there were so many suspects, and Adam didn't know much about any of them. "I wonder if it'll happen again."

"I don't know," Gavin said.

"I mean, that money needs to go toward the fire company. A fire could strike at any time." He glanced at Zeph, shuddering at what he learned about pets suffocating in house fires. "Who would steal from a volunteer fire company?"

The line went silent for a moment. "So who is Patrick?" Gavin asked finally.

"Huh?"

"When I called, you thought I was someone named Patrick."

"Oh. Patrick's my best friend. We play baseball together. His dad's the coach, and the two of them are really serious about it. Pat's training all winter, which is why he's not volunteering with me."

"Oh." Gavin sounded sad.

"You'd probably like him. Maybe I can have a sleepover—you, me, and him. I'll ask my parents."

"That would be cool."

"Pizza, video games, and comic books. Some of my favorite things," Adam agreed. "If you come over, you have to read about Riley Couth. You don't know what you're missing. Oh, and then there's Logan Zephyr and the Stellar Squadron if you like stories about outer space."

"Sounds fun." Gavin sighed. "I can't wait." He paused.

Adam wrote *Gavin—sad?* in his notebook.

"Well," Gavin said finally. "I guess I'll see you tomorrow."

"Yep."

"Bye, Adam."

"Bye, Gavin."

Adam hung up the phone and turned around. Zeph had moved into Sapphie's pink princess bed for a nap. "Oh, Zeph," Adam sighed. "You'll never sleep in the rocketship bed I got for you, will you?"

Zeph sat up and howled.

"Come here, boy."

Zeph pranced over to Adam, who knelt down to scratch his ears. "If I have a sleepover, you can stay up with me all night. Would you like that?"

"Arooo!" Zeph howled, wagging his tail.

"I'm sure glad you're a good dog, not like Sapphie. You're so good, I bet you could pass that obedience class without any effort at all."

"Arooo!" Zeph answered.

"All right." Adam sat on the floor and tapped the floor for Zeph to sit next to him. "Get out of that princess bed and get comfortable. We've got a lot of reading to finish before dinner."

~ Five ~

That evening, as the Hollingers enjoyed pizza on the couch while watching a movie, Zeph and Sapphie snuggled together in Zeph's rocketship bed.

Zeph whined into Sapphie's ear. "Don't leave again. You shouldn't run off by yourself."

"I have to."

"Please, Sapphie." Zeph pawed her ear. "I miss you when you're gone, and I worry."

"Oh, Zeph, you do nothing but worry even when I'm here."

"Please stay."

"Hmph!" Sapphie spun around and pressed into the middle of the bed, pushing Zeph to the side. "You sound just like Sir. Stay this, stay that."

"Who's Sir?"

"This Person Courtney takes me to. He's so bossy and sneaky, telling me to sit, stay, come, down. And he's tricky, too. It's not fair. When he tells me something, I have to obey, obey, *obey*! It's like I don't even get a choice in the matter. It's bad, bad, *bad*!"

"Sapphie, be quiet," Courtney called. "We're trying to watch a movie!"

"Fine!" Sapphie yipped before turning to her brother and speaking more quietly. "Anyway, at least I'm learning how to train Courtney."

"What?"

"There are these things Sir is trying to teach her, but she isn't very good at learning them, so I'm learning to train her instead."

"How?"

"At the class, there are these little squares we're supposed to sit on. They're soft and springy and good to chew on. When I want to play on one of the squares, all I do is cock my head, paw at her leg, and pull toward the square. And like magic, Courtney follows."

"What does Sir think of that?"

Sapphie rolled toward Zeph to grab his ear. "Sir doesn't like it one bit. But that doesn't matter. He's only in charge at the class. That's where he lives."

Zeph pulled his ear away from his sister's sharp teeth. "I think I like this 'Sir' Person."

"You *would* like him, Zeph. He's all rules and no fun. You'd get a bacon strip for sure."

"Bacon strip?"

"It's a special treat Sir gives to dogs who are boring like you. He gives them out the whole class."

"They sound yummy. I wondered if I smelled bacon this evening. I thought it might be the pizza."

Sapphie's eye bulged open. "Bacon pizza? I didn't know they made such a thing. I want some now, now, *now*!"

Four voices from the couch called, "Shhh!"

Sapphie snuggled against Zeph.

"Are they delicious?" Zeph asked.

"Are what delicious?"

"The bacon treats."

"Oh, those. Of course. They're bacon—duh!"

Zeph licked his lips. "Are they filling?"

"I don't know," said Sapphie.

"How could you not know?" Sapphie looked away. "Oh." Zeph licked her ear. "Were you not good enough to receive a treat from Sir?"

Sapphie growled.

Zeph cowered. "Just promise you won't run away again."

Sapphie answered with another growl. "I promise nothing." She pounced at Zeph, who dashed away into Sapphie's pink princess bed. Sapphie curled up in Zephs' rocketship bed, but after a minute or two, she stood up, crept over, and snuggled next to Zeph in the princess bed, so close and warm and cuddly that he could feel her heartbeat right next to his for the rest of the evening.

~ * ~

That night, Courtney spoke softly to Sapphie as she tucked her into her crate.

"Mom thinks you've been getting better at class, Sapphie." Courtney patted her. "I hope she's right. She thinks tomorrow I can finally take you to volunteer with me at the nursing home. Would you like that?"

Sapphie spun in her crate, barking once.

"Mom thinks that if I spend more time with you, you won't run away any more. Is that true?"

Sapphie cocked her head.

"Rest up, then." Courtney closed the door, securing the latch. "Tomorrow will be a busy day."

When Courtney turned out the kitchen light and went upstairs, Sapphie turned to face her brother's crate. "Zeph, what's a nursing home?"

Zeph sat up. "I'm not sure."

"What's a kang-arooo?" she asked, remembering the strange word from earlier.

"I don't know."

She whined. "Zeph, I thought you knew everything!"

Zeph turned around three times and then snuggled into his blanket. "I'll try to find out for you."

"Do you think I'll like it?"

"Like what? A kang-arooo?"

Sapphie barked. "*I'm* the kang-arooo! Don't you pay attention to anything, Zeph?"

"What?"

"They called me a kang-arooo. It must be like a princess or something."

Zeph sighed. "I'm not so sure."

"Nevermind about the kang-arooo, then. Do you think I'll like a nursing home? Do you think maybe it tastes like bacon? Do you think it's something I can chase?"

"I don't think it's either of those things, Sapphie. I think it's a place, and I think I like it already."

Sapphie jumped up. "Why?"

Zeph turned around three times again, trying to find the perfect spot for sleeping. "Because if you go to the nursing home with your Person, it means you won't have time to escape."

"Hmph! I hadn't thought of that." Saphie clawed at her cage, but Zeph was already falling asleep. No matter. She'd show everyone. If she really wanted to escape, she'd escape. And no person or animal—not even Sir—would stop her.

She looked up at the moonlight coming in through the window and felt the puff of warm air coming up through the heating vents. It was a cold night out there in the woods—even for Shadow. She could escape if she really wanted to. But she curled up in her comfy crate, enjoying the warmth of her people's house. She realized that for tonight, she didn't want to escape at all.

~ Six ~

Courtney glared at the sign: Willow Lakes Retirement Living and Nursing Home. A cool autumn breeze blew the leaves in a small whirlwind, and Courtney shivered. She had been there twice already, and she dreaded each time. So far, Mom had done much of the talking. Courtney didn't know what to say to old people. It's not like they had anything in common with her.

She followed Mom into the building and bit her lip. The nursing home always smelled like medicine and old people. She couldn't believe her parents set no end date for her punishment, even though she'd only been ordered to serve forty hours. She'd probably be volunteering here for the next three hundred years!

Courtney held Sapphie in her arms, following Mom into the lobby.

"Put Sapphie down," Mom said. "That way you can write your name on the volunteer sign-in sheet."

"It's not volunteering if I'm being forced," Courtney muttered.

"What was that?"

"Nothing, Mom. I mean—Sapphie's not clipped to her leash. She might run off."

Mom smiled. "She'll be fine. Her training's going well. She'll listen to you. Keep your instructor's words in mind: have confidence, and Sapphie will follow you."

Courtney put Sapphie down and tried to feel confident as she walked to the reception desk.

The receptionist, Mrs. Bowers, smiled at her. "Good morning, Courtney."

"Good morning, Mrs. Bowers."

The woman smiled with a wide, happy, contagious grin. Courtney couldn't help but smile back. Mrs. Bowers flashed a sparkly pink wave. Her manicure complimented her pink stockings, a pink skirt, a light pink blouse, a neon pink pin in the shape of a star, and dangling pink flamingo earrings. On her desk sat a cell phone with a pink rhinestone case. It reminded Courtney of her own cell phone, which her parents had taken away after the incident at Halloween.

That was the only good part about volunteering at the nursing home. As a reward, Courtney was given back her cell phone to use from Saturday afternoon until Sunday evening.

"I think it's so nice of you to spend your Saturday mornings here." Mrs. Bowers beamed. "You have no idea how much your visits mean to the residents." She held out a pink flamingo pen for Courtney to sign with. Sapphie squealed and jumped into the air, snapping at the pen.

Mrs. Bowers clapped her hands and smiled even wider. "My word! What a cute puppy!"

"Sapphie, down." Courtney clapped her hand the way her instructor taught her.

Sapphie sat with a reluctant growl. Courtney took the pen and signed her name quickly, watching as Sapphie eyed the pen.

"This is Sapphie. She's my puppy, and she's going to come around to visit the residents with me today."

Mrs. Bowers rushed around to the front of the desk and knelt down. "She's adorable! She's an absolute princess, ain't she?"

"Isn't she," Mom corrected in a whisper.

Sapphie wagged her tail and plopped onto the ground, belly up, so that Mrs. Bowers could more easily pet her.

Mom smiled. "She certainly likes you. She doesn't behave this well with just anyone."

"Dogs always love me." Mrs. Bowers smiled. "I used to have several dogs. Now, though, with my aching joints, I'm just not in shape to look after a dog."

"What about cats?" Mom asked.

"Maybe." Mrs. Bowers stopped rubbing Sapphie's

belly, and Sapphie sat up, barking twice.

"Quiet, Sapphie."

"Oh, she just wants more attention." Mrs. Bowers smiled at the puppy. "She'll love all the attention she gets from residents. My, how she'll brighten their day!"

Mom looked at her watch. "I guess I'll go run some errands, and I'll be back to pick you up in a bit."

"You're leaving?"

Mom nodded. "You've been here a few times already. I think you're old enough to stay here on your own." Courtney eyed the clock. She had been signed in for three minutes already. Fifty-seven more to go. Without Mom, what in the world was she going to talk to the residents about? She watched as Mom and Mrs. Bowers exchanged glances. Some type of secret adult communication. Probably, they were happy to see her squirm. Mom handed Courtney a leash and then walked out the door. Courtney sighed and led Sapphie down the hall, hoping the rest of the hour would pass quickly.

Sapphie paused, her nose twitching. Then she ran off in the direction of whatever she smelled. Courtney gulped and followed Sapphie to the cafeteria.

Residents sat at round tables, each one with a small vase of flowers at the center. This time they were orange and yellow, colors of Thanksgiving. Some residents sat in wheelchairs, others sat with canes. Some didn't look too old at all—kind of like Courtney's grandmother.

Sapphie's nose still twitched—today's lunch smelled like roast beef and potatoes—and Courtney clipped on her leash and held it tightly. As she walked toward the window, Sapphie howled a gritty little *roar*. The chatter of the lunchroom silenced, and all eyes turned to Sapphie.

She stood facing Mr. Grindle, who sat at a table with his cane leaning against his chair. The hair raised on Sapphie's shackles. She continued growling. All eyes—dozens of diners—continued to stare, and Courtney felt her face flush.

"Sapphie, stop!" Courtney shrieked.

But Sapphie continued her growls.

"It's the cane," Courtney explained. She picked up the squirming puppy and shielded her from the cane.

"She's afraid of canes?" asked Mr. Grindle.

"There was a bad man in our neighborhood this summer. He walked with a cane—or, at least, he pretended to. He hurt our dogs." Courtney leaned closer to Sapphie's ear. "Sapphie, this is Mister Grindle. He's a nice man. Mister Grindle is good. He lives here."

The old man laughed. "I'll get her to like me, alright." He turned to his plate and scooped up a giant spoonful of brown mush. Then he turned back to Courtney and winked, dropping the scoop on the floor. It fell with a moist *plop*. Sapphie squirmed out of Courtney's arms and lunged for the food. She ate it in less than two seconds.

Mr. Grindle laughed.

A small old woman who sat next to him snickered. "You aren't s'pposed to drop food like that. You're gonna get in trouble, Peter Grindle!"

He wagged a crooked finger at her. "You worry too much, Eleanor Grindle."

The old woman crossed her arms. "You'll get in trouble, I say."

Mr. Grindle laughed. "Maybe I will. Maybe I won't." He turned to Courtney. "My wife has been worrying about me for more than fifty years now. Thing is, I don't like meatloaf. And look at that puppy. She loves it!"

Indeed, Sapphie was seated diligently at Mr. Grindle's feet, drooling.

"Here ya go, pup." He dropped another spoonful.

Old Mrs. Grindle tapped the table. "That's not meatloaf. That's roast beef. You're supposed to eat it. Otherwise, you'll be hungry tonight."

Mr. Grindle turned back to Courtney and winked. "Ever get tired of being told what to do?"

Courtney nodded.

"Me, too." He dropped another spoonful, which Sapphie devoured. "It tastes like meatloaf to me. See how they mash up all my food so I can eat it?" He smiled at Courtney with a toothless grin. "Got all my teeth pulled out years ago. Now I can't chew. I never thought much of brushing my teeth, but you know how that saying goes: you don't miss something until it's gone."

Courtney knelt down to pet Sapphie. She nodded at Mr. Grindle, thinking about how worried she had been when Sapphie went missing. Mr. Grindle winked at Courtney again and dropped another spoonful, which Sapphie lapped up.

"Better stop," Courtney whispered. She pointed to Miss Betty, one of the nurses at the other side of the cafeteria. "She's been watching you, and she's headed our way."

Miss Betty hurried over and crossed her arms with determination. "Now Mister Grindle, why are you dropping your food on the floor? You know food only does you good if it lands in your stomach."

Mr. Grindle crossed his arms, too. "I *hate* meatloaf."

"Mister Grindle, it's roast beef, not meatloaf."

"Tastes like meatloaf to me. All mushed up like mashed potatoes."

"Now, you know the only reason you have to get your food all mushed up like that is because you refuse to wear your dentures."

"I *hate* dentures." Mr. Grindle's eyes sparkled, and he dropped another spoonful of mushy meat onto the floor. Miss Betty's eyes flashed with shock, and Mr. Grindle chuckled. Courtney tried not to laugh.

Miss Betty looked down at Sapphie. "Even if you don't want the food yourself, you've given that dog an awful lot of meat. Do you see how tiny she is? You might make her sick."

Mr. Grindle didn't respond. Instead, he forced himself to eat two spoonfuls of meat. Miss Betty nodded. "That's better, Mister Grindle." She patted him on the shoulder before moving to another table.

Mr. Grindle winked at Courtney. Then he picked up his plate and scraped its entire contents onto the floor. Sapphie's eyes bulged out larger than Courtney had ever seen them. The puppy lunged at the pile of food, slurping it with loud, gurgling gulps.

Courtney couldn't help but burst out laughing, and Mr. Grindle joined in. Even his wife, sitting next to him, joined in the laughter. Miss Betty shot them a mean look from across the room, but luckily, she didn't return.

When Courtney finally controlled her laughter, she turned to Mr. Grindle. "I didn't know old people actually break the rules." She blushed. "Sorry, I didn't mean to call you old."

He placed his plate on the floor and watched Sapphie lick it clean. "Young lady, we've got over seven decades' worth of experience breaking rules compared to you young people."

Mrs. Grindle finished chuckling. "That's always the way with you young folks. You always think you're the only ones to break the rules. But remember, old people used to be young people, too. Folks have been breaking rules forever. It's human nature."

Courtney sighed. "Tell that to my mom."

Mrs. Grindle's face grew serious. "I'm not saying it's *good* to break the rules."

Mr. Grindle sipped some water. "Of course, Eleanor has never broke a rule in her life. Always obeys. Always over-achieving." He reached over and patted his wife's hand with his own.

"Sounds like my brother." Courtney smiled. "He's a Goody Two-Shoes. Never breaks the rules, always does his homework, nice to everyone, loved by all his teachers. I never understand how he can be so good all the time."

Mr. Grindle smiled at his wife. "It takes all kinds of people to make the world go 'round. If everyone acted as good as your brother or my wife, the world would be a boring place. If everyone always broke the rules like me—"

"Or like me," Courtney added.

Mr. Grindle nodded. "If that were the case, then the world would be chaotic. Nothing would ever get done. Can you imagine if all the diners dumped their food onto the floor?"

Courtney looked around. There were at least a dozen people eating, and Courtney tried to imagine that much food sitting on the floor. "Sapphie would be happy. It would probably take her a whole two minutes to eat it all."

Mr. Grindle looked down at Sapphie. She wagged her tail and barked. Mr. Grindle laughed. "She's got a spark in her, alright. Keep your eye on that one."

Sapphie barked again. Then she backed up and took a running leap, bounding off the wheel of Mrs. Grindle's wheelchair and landing on Mr. Grindle's lap.

"Oh, sorry." Courtney reached for Sapphie.

"It's okay." Sapphie had already curled up in Mr. Grindle's lap, and he scratched behind her ears. "We can let her stay for a while—until Miss Betty yells at me."

"He loves dogs," Mrs. Grindle added. "He's had dogs all his life, 'til a few years before we moved in here."

"I'm glad you brought her." Mr. Grindle smiled. "Are you here visiting a grandparent?"

"No. I'm volunteering. Or, um, maybe I'm being forced to volunteer. I did some dumb stuff this Halloween, and I wasn't taking good enough care of Sapphie. So now I have to take her to obedience school, and as for me—well, it's a long story."

Mr. Grindle shrugged. "I've got time. I'd love to hear it."

Courtney pulled up a chair. With Sapphie sleeping on Mr. Grindle's lap, Courtney started her tale, beginning with the day Mom got lost coming home from the mall and ended up on a farm with four corgi puppies for sale. By the time she got to the part about JJ and her nasty Halloween trick on her brother, Mom had returned.

"There you are, Courtney." Mom took a look at

sleeping Sapphie. "I looked all over for you. Mrs. Bowers said you came here first, but I didn't think you'd still be in the cafeteria. And look at Sapphie. I've never seen her sleep so soundly."

"Stomach's full," Mr. Grindle said.

Mom raised an eyebrow.

"Long story," Courtney said. "You remember Mister and Mrs. Grindle?"

Mom shook hands. "We met briefly last weekend."

"Lovely daughter you have there," Mr. Grindle said.

"Very kind," Mrs. Grindle agreed.

Mom raised another eyebrow.

"Long story," Courtney said again.

"You can tell me in the car." Mom smiled at the old couple. "I'm sure Courtney will be back to visit next week. Sapphie, wake up. It's time to go."

Sapphie sat up groggily, licking her lips. She took one look at Mom and Courtney before snuggling back into Mr. Grindle's lap. Courtney sighed and picked her up.

"Sapphie, time for a ride in the car!"

Sapphie snapped awake, wagging her whole body so fast that Courtney almost dropped her. Courtney placed her on the floor and held the leash tightly as Sapphie bolted for the door.

Courtney paused near Mom's minivan. "We'd better see if she has to go first. She might have, um, eaten a lot."

"Eaten?"

"It's a long story, Mom. But trust me—your car will thank me later."

In the car, a few minutes later, Mom turned to Courtney. "I'm proud of you, you know."

"Why?"

"You were very nice in there. You made their day, visiting with Mister and Mrs. Grindle. And you had Sapphie under control, too."

Courtney smiled.

"And, of course, since it's Saturday afternoon..."

Mom reached into her pocketbook. Courtney's eyes flashed. She'd almost forgotten about her cell phone.

Mom smiled. "I charged it for you last night."

Courtney took the phone and felt the bumpy rhinestone pattern as it slipped into the familiar spot in her palm. She powered on the phone, and while she waited for it to load, she told Mom all about Mr. Grindle and what he did with his lunch.

"Sounds like you made a new friend today." Mom smiled. "I'm proud of you, Courtney." She turned back to the road.

Courtney looked down at her phone. Several new text messages awaited her:

> **Aileen:** TXT me when u get this.
> **Noelle:** Saturday seems so far awaaay! txt when ur parents give ur phone back
> **Meghan:** Lots 2 discuss. How was volunteering?

Courtney sent a text to Aileen. It felt good to hold the phone again in her hand, and her fingers remembered exactly how to text:

> **Courtney:** Nice 2 have phone back. Volunteering wasn't bad.
> **Aileen:** Rly?
> **Courtney:** Met a nice old guy who seems like he was cool when younger. Feels like I made a new friend.
> **Aileen:** Old ppl? Lame. Noelle and Meghan are here w/me. When will u b ungrounded?
> **Courtney:** Maybe never. But mom was proud of me 2day, so soon, maybe?
> **Aileen:** Lame. Nice job acting. Can't wait 2 hang out.

Courtney wanted to type, "I wasn't acting." She wasn't, after all. Mr. Grindle *was* a nice guy. Volunteering wasn't really all that bad, and the hour flew by. But she didn't want her friends to think she was turning into a dork. So instead, she changed the subject:

Courtney: There's a play at school this month. I'm
             auditioning. Want to?
Aileen: Kinda dorky.

So much for escaping the label of "dork."

Aileen: Noelle says she can never memorize lines.
Aileen: Meghan says when r rehearsals?
Courtney: After school.
Aileen: Meghan says she needs after school time 2
             unwind.

Courtney frowned, thinking that if Meghan didn't keep busy enough, she might get into trouble like her older brother, JJ.

Aileen: Count us all out.
Courtney: :(
Aileen: Court, don't turn into ur brother, k?
Courtney: ??
Aileen: Don't be all dorky and goody-goody all the
             time.
Courtney: K.
Aileen: We're at the movies now, so got 2 go. 2 bad
             ur grounded. C-ya.
Courtney: Okay :(Have fun.

The texts stopped.

Courtney stared out the window as her mom drove. She thought about going to the movies with her friends and tried to imagine all the fun she'd be missing, but her mind kept wandering to the upcoming play, and she couldn't wait for auditions.

In fact, she might even stop by Cassie's house to find out a little more about the play. She looked down at her phone and couldn't help the sinking feeling in her stomach. She tried to remember why she liked her phone so much, but her days of texting and hanging out with JJ—even though only a couple of weeks ago—seemed like a different lifetime.

~ Seven ~

When Adam arrived at the fire hall, all the wedding decorations had been put away. The dance floor was now covered with rows of long tables. Each was covered in a plain paper tablecloth with a large number drawn in the middle.

Spencer stood at the large window that opened to the kitchen. He held a clipboard. Behind him, huge pots of water steamed, enveloping the kitchen in a foggy mist. Adam heard the sound of boiling water and smelled meatballs simmering in tomato sauce. His stomach growled. Though volunteers were allowed to eat, they had to wait for a free moment.

Spencer checked his watch. "Hollinger, Adam." He marked the clipboard. "You're on time. Your buddy Gavin is not."

"That's because my dad drove me." Adam smiled. "See, my mom is always late. If it's not getting lost, it's getting distracted by bad grammar..." But Adam's smile faded when Spencer rolled his eyes.

"You're the first one here, Hollinger. Everyone else is late."

"Who else is coming?"

"Besides Gavin, Bill will be here. And Spark. And the grown-ups, of course."

"No Emily?"

"No. She worked this morning, cleaning up from the wedding."

"Oh." Adam frowned. "Well, what should I do?"

"We have to complete all these tasks before the guests arrive." He held out his clipboard. "You can go into the men's bathroom. Make sure both paper towel dispensers are full. Then check all the toilet paper holders. There are extra supplies in the cabinet below the sinks.

You do know how to change a paper towel roll, right?"

Adam nodded.

"Good. Off you go."

Adam hurried toward the bathroom, eager to be away from Spencer. There was just something about him. He enjoyed being in charge way too much. Adam took his time in the bathroom, hoping that Gavin would be there by the time he finished. He hoped they could work together.

When Adam returned to the fire hall, Gavin was lining the four large trash cans with black trash bags. Adam helped him with the last one.

"Sorry I'm late." Gavin looked to make sure Spencer wasn't watching. "My mom's car has trouble starting sometimes. Something's wrong with the starter, or maybe the ignition switch, or the alternator. That's what the mechanic said, anyway. But Mom says it's too expensive to fix right now. We're supposed to be flying to my cousin's house for Thanksgiving, and she says it's either buying the plane tickets or fixing the car."

Adam frowned. "I would think fixing the car would be more important."

"That's true, but she doesn't want our cousins to think we don't have money."

"Oh." Adam had never even heard of a starter, an ignition switch, or an alternator, but they sounded expensive. His parents had brought their cars to the shop for repairs before, but they never talked about any of the details—including the cost.

Gavin sighed. "My dad bought a restaurant a little while ago, and business is a little slow. He keeps saying things will pick up, though."

"What kind of—"

"Adam! Gavin!" Both boys turned to see Spencer staring at them, tapping his foot. They turned to him.

"No time for chit-chat, boys. We've got work to do. See that big table in the middle of the room? The one with the empty bins?"

The boys nodded.

"I need you to fill the bins. They're all labeled: butter, salt, pepper, forks, knives, and spoons. And a napkin dispenser. The plasticware and napkins are above the coat racks. You'll have to get the stepladder out of the kitchen to reach it. The butter, salt, and pepper packets are in the cabinet in the hallway that leads to the kitchen. Got it?"

Both boys nodded. Even if he didn't get it, Adam wouldn't have felt comfortable asking questions. Instead, he walked toward the kitchen. Gavin followed.

"Stepladder first, then plasticware."

Gavin cleared his throat. "I heard Chief Kurle talking on the way in. He said it's a pretty full house tonight— considering."

"Considering what?" Adam reached the stepladder first. It was almost as tall as him. He took one end, and Gavin took the other. They headed toward the coat room.

"Considering it's only a spaghetti dinner." Gavin stumbled a bit, and Adam shifted the ladder's weight. "Chief Kurle says the big seller is the crab feed. They have one each month. But he said tonight is almost as busy."

"I guess we'd better get plenty of supplies, then."

They arrived in the coat room and positioned the stepladder under the shelf. Adam looked up.

"I'll climb and hand the box down to you."

Gavin nodded. "When do you think we get to eat?"

Adam handed down a box of plastic forks. "Not sure. I guess whenever there's some down time."

"I hope it's soon. I'm hungry."

"Me, too." Adam handed down the spoons, knives, and napkins, one box at a time. "Now what?" he asked.

"I'll go get the bins from the table out there. We'll fill them here and then bring them back out."

"Good thinking." While Gavin returned to the main dining hall, Adam looked around. There were only a few coats so far—Adam's, Gavin's, Spencer's, and some of the adults'. His stomach rumbled, but he knew it was only partly from hunger. He also worried about volunteering with all the diners around. What if he messed up? What if he forgot what he was supposed to do? Spencer didn't seem too forgiving.

Gavin returned with the bins, stacked one inside the other. His face was flushed.

"You okay?" Adam asked.

"Yes, but Spencer saw me. He said we're taking too long."

"Huh?"

Gavin pointed to the door at the end of the coat room. "The guests all enter through that door, hang their coats up, and then go into the dining hall. Spencer said the doors are supposed to open in six minutes, and with the stepladder out and the boxes on the floor, we're in the way."

"Better hurry, then."

Adam opened the box of plastic forks and scooped several handfuls into the bin marked "forks." Gavin neatly stacked the napkins into the napkin dispenser. They hurried to the serving table, placed the napkins and forks, and raced back.

"Knives and spoons," Adam said, and the boys scooped knives and spoons into the bins as quickly as possible. They hurried back out to the table in the dining hall and rushed back to the coat room. Adam climbed the ladder, and Gavin handed him the boxes of unused forks, spoons, knives, and napkins.

Just as the clock in the dining hall chimed six o'clock, Adam climbed down the ladder and gave Gavin a high-five.

"We did it before—"

But he didn't get to finish: Spencer had arrived.

"You're slow," he announced.

Adam and Gavin averted their eyes. "It's our first time," Gavin whispered.

"I'm opening the door in thirty seconds. That means you have fifteen seconds to get the stepladder out of the way."

The boys moved faster than they ever moved in baseball or gym, bringing the ladder back to the kitchen.

"That was close," Adam panted.

Gavin sighed. "He doesn't have to be so mean."

"He's too bossy. He reminds me of this guy my sister used to—never mind. We should get—"

"The butter, salt, and pepper. And before Spencer comes back!"

The bins for butter, salt, and pepper packets were smaller and easier to fill, and the boys finished in no time. They reported back to the window in front of the kitchen, where Spencer stood with his clipboard, surveying the entire dining hall.

"We're all done," Gavin announced with a smile.

"You think so?" Spencer tapped his clipboard.

Adam nodded. "We were wondering when we would be able to eat."

Spencer snickered. "Since you two will be collecting tickets from diners, you'll have to wait until everyone's been served. We start serving at six-thirty, but there's something you need to fix before then."

"Fix?"

"You boys take a look at the table you set up and fix it—immediately. I would have thought a fourth and a fifth grader would be smarter than that."

Adam and Gavin hurried to the table. Adam wondered what was wrong. Everything seemed fine. The napkins were in the napkin bin, the forks were in the fork bin—

Gavin started laughing.

Adam squinted at the table. "What?"

"See what we did?" Gavin giggled.

When Adam looked again, he giggled, too. They had put the spoons in the bin labeled "knives" and the knives in the bin labeled "spoons."

"Guess we were in too much of a rush," Adam said while they fixed their mistake.

"At least we got out of the way before everyone arrived."

The dining hall was filling quickly with diners. A few were already heading toward the center table to get plasticware and napkins, so Adam and Gavin hurried to the back of the room. There, carrying a large, shiny metal bowl, a sheet of paper, and a marker, was Spark. Just like last time, she wore a bright red t-shirt with her Stoney Brook Fire Company jacket blazing.

"Look at you two." Spark snickered.

Adam and Gavin shrugged. "What about us?"

Her face looked serious. "You don't look like official volunteers."

"Why not?" Adam frowned.

Spark squinted at them for as long as she could stand it. Then, her face broke into a smile and she giggled. "You don't look like official volunteers because you aren't wearing the right gear."

She reached into the large bowl and produced two bright red t-shirts, handing one to each boy. "These are official Stoney Brook Fire Company t-shirts. You should wear them every time you volunteer." She spun around to model the identical t-shirt she wore. She smiled again. "Welcome to the fire company, boys. Now if you'll excuse me, I have to go make the numbers for the table raffle."

"Table raffle?" Gavin asked, but Spark had already hurried off.

"I remember from when I ate here with my family. There's always someone who chooses numbers out of a hat—or a bowl—to see which table gets in line first. First in line, first to eat. The time I came here, we were almost the last table. I must have been bad luck or something!"

Gavin nodded and held up his t-shirt. "Let's go put these on."

The boys walked to the bathroom to change into their shirts. Adam walked slowly to catch his breath from all the running around. He thought about Riley Couth, who always warned against rushing. Rushing only led to messes—like mixing up knives and spoons—and to misreading important clues. If money really did go missing from the fire hall, Adam would have to stop rushing around so much and start paying more attention.

"Hey, Adam?" Gavin asked.

"Yes?"

"Nothing."

They turned around, glancing at their shirts in the mirror.

"We look awesome!" Gavin said.

"We do!" Adam looked at his reflection. The bright red shirt reminded him of his Lancaster Reds uniform, and for a minute, he missed baseball and Patrick and couldn't wait for his favorite time of year to return.

"Hey, Adam?" Gavin scratched his head.

"Yes?"

"I was thinking..."

Adam raised an eyebrow.

"I was just thinking about what you said—having a sleepover with me and your friend Patrick. Do you still..."

"Oh yeah. I almost forgot. I'll ask my mom tonight, and if she says it's okay, I'll call you and Patrick in the morning."

Gavin's face stretched into a smile. "Cool."

Adam took one last look in the mirror. "Ready?"

"Ready."

As soon as the boys entered the dining hall, Spencer waved at them. They hurried over.

"Okay, boys. I get to go around selling candy bars this time. Fire Chief Kurle says I get to collect the money." He motioned to the corner of the room, where Bill was slicing open a large box of candy bars with a utility knife. "Bill will be helping me by carrying the boxes around." He handed Gavin a large, shiny metal bowl—like the one Spark carried. "I need the two of you to stand in front of this buffet table. In about fifteen minutes, the grown-ups will fill the buffet table with plates of spaghetti, baskets of dinner rolls, and bowls of Italian wedding soup. The diners will form a line. When they do, Adam can tear their ticket in half. Give half to Gavin to keep in the bowl. No ticket, no food. Got it?"

They nodded.

"After that, once everyone has been served, the two of you can eat. There's a small table for volunteers set up in the back of the kitchen. When you're done eating, come back out and empty any trash bags that are full. Take them out to the dumpster. Remember where that is?"

"Yes."

"Okay, boys." Spencer hung his clipboard on a peg on the wall and picked up a large glass jar that was sitting on the buffet table. Then he made his way over to Bill, and the two teenagers walked around the tables, talking to diners.

Gavin watched them. "Do you think we'll act like that when we're teenagers?"

"Like what?"

Spencer and Bill looked like they were joking around whenever no one was watching. They were laughing and patting each other on the back after each sale. A few of the diners even looked uncomfortable.

Adam sighed, thinking of his sister's friends. "I've seen some crazy teenagers, and I don't think we'll ever act like that."

"I hope not." Gavin sighed. "My cousin's a teenager, though, and he's pretty wild sometimes."

"Is this the cousin you might visit at Thanksgiving?"

"Yep."

Adam squinted at Spencer and Bill, watching them stuff the money into the jar. His head tingled, and he wished he were wearing his detective fedora. Could someone as serious as Spencer be involved in stealing money from the fire company? Adam turned back to Gavin. "What kind of crazy stuff does your cousin do?"

"He's very energetic. If he's not playing sports, he's completely restless. Oh, and he never stops eating. And he's oblivious, too. Or maybe clumsy. He's always knocking things over while practicing football plays inside the house."

"I'm sure there are teenagers who are normal."

"Maybe crazy is normal for teenagers. I don't know any teenagers who are normal."

Adam thought back to the names he'd listed in his notebook. "What about Emily? She's a teenager, and she seems down to earth."

"That's true."

The dining hall was getting full, and the low hum of conversation had risen. The boys had to raise their voices to hear each other.

"I asked my mom about getting some of those Riley Couth comic books."

"And?"

"She says we can't afford them right now, but maybe for my birthday. Or Christmas—it's just a month and a half away."

"When's your birthday?"

"March."

Adam nodded. "You can read mine at the sleepover."

Gavin smiled.

A loud, sharp voice cut through the chatter. Adam and Gavin looked up to see Spark standing at the table in the corner—the one that held the raffle tickets—with a microphone. She stood tall and confident, blazing in her red fire company gear. "Welcome, ladies and gentlemen, to the Stoney Brook Fire Company's November Fifteenth Spaghetti Dinner Night!"

"I wish I was as confident as her," Gavin muttered.

"Me, too."

Spark continued. "I'll be randomly selecting table numbers from this bowl. When I call your table's number, please make your way to the two young gentlemen near the buffet table."

All the diners searched for Adam and Gavin.

"Wave, boys," Spark said into the microphone.

Adam felt his ears burn as he and Gavin waved to the entire room of diners.

"They'll be collecting your tickets. Once they do, you can make your way to the table and help yourself to soup, rolls, and pasta. The meatballs are especially delicious, cooked by my dad, Paul Harper. Take all you want, but eat all you take. After everyone has been served, you may go up for seconds." She reached into the bowl. "Aaaand...the first table to get in line for food is..."

The entire room held its breath.

"Table number seven!"

The room erupted in both sighs and cheers as the diners seated at table seven stood and walked toward Adam and Gavin.

"Here we go," Adam said.

The diners passed by quickly. Adam took their tickets, tore them in half, and put the ticket stub in Gavin's bowl. Every once in a while, Gavin said "enjoy your meal." Adam couldn't think of anything to say except "thank you."

One of the diners, a man with a blue baseball cap, stopped when he saw Adam.

"Thank you," Adam said, taking his ticket.

"You're the pitcher, aren't you?"

Adam felt his ears burn. He nodded.

The man turned to his wife. "Honey, this is that pitcher from the summer. Remember? He pitched in the Autumn League. There was a write-up about him in the sports section of the paper." He turned back to Adam. "Congratulations, kid."

"Thanks."

"Wow," Gavin said as he held up the bowl to collect ticket stubs. "I didn't know you pitched for Autumn League. All I can say is—wow!"

"We didn't win," Adam said.

"It doesn't matter. Just making the team is awesome. Only the best play post-season." Gavin's eyes turned watery and dreamy. "Sometimes I wish I played sports."

Adam turned to Gavin. "Maybe next spring you can—"

Spark's voice echoed through the microphone. "The next table to get in line for food is...table number nine!"

Once again, the room erupted in both sighs and cheers as the hungry diners at table nine lined up. As more and more people stood in line, Adam and Gavin had less time to talk. Adam kept his eye lowered, trying not to attract any additional attention.

Just as the last set of tables lined up, Chief Kurle approached the boys. "How are my newest volunteers doing?"

"We're doing good," Gavin said.

Adam nodded.

"Looks like you're finding your way around pretty well." Kurle smiled. "Packed house tonight. More people means more money for the fire company. Think of all the equipment we can replace." He stared dreamily at the diners.

Adam nodded again but tried to focus on collecting tickets. He looked up to take a ticket from a table eleven diner. "I tell ya," the man said, "I'm always at the last table to go up! I must be bad luck or s—" He cocked his head. "Hey, I know you! You're that boy from the newspaper."

"The pitcher," Gavin explained.

"What pitcher?" The diner rubbed his chin. "No, I'm talking about the hero. The boy with the dog. The one who found the burglar over the summer." The diner turned to

Kurle. "You're lucky to have such an accomplished young volunteer. Do you know he's a crime fighter at age ten?"

The man patted Adam on the back before continuing on to his food. Adam peeked over to see Chief Kurle smiling wide. Adam wondered what was redder—his shirt, or his red, throbbing ears.

Adam looked over at Gavin. His eyes widened. "You found a burglar?"

Adam nodded. "With the help of Zeph, my dog. And I guess my sister's dog helped a little, too."

"Oh, man, that's so cool." Gavin smiled, but his smile faded. "I wish we had a dog, but my parents said with the restaurant, we wouldn't have time to let it out or walk it or anything."

"You can play with Zeph when you come to my house." Adam continued tearing the last few tickets, hoping his ears would cool back to normal.

When the last of the diners went through the line, Gavin breathed a sigh of relief. "We did it, Adam." He smiled, holding up the big bowl. "We got everyone through the line. Everyone looks happy, and the food must be good—it's so quiet!"

Adam looked around and noticed that most diners were eating. "I guess we can eat now, too."

"That's right, boys," said a booming voice behind them. Adam turned around to see that Chief Kurle was still there. He had been watching the boys for several minutes. "I'm gonna join ya, if you don't mind. I heard about the boy with the dog over the summer. I just got an idea, and I want to talk about it with you."

Adam followed the chief to the buffet table. He grabbed a heaping plate of spaghetti smothered in sauce and meatballs, and he took three rolls—his favorite. He skipped the soup. With all the embarrassing talk about his accomplishments, his ears were hot enough.

In the back of the kitchen, he sat at a table with Gavin and Chief Kurle.

"Oh, we forgot plasticware and butter," Gavin said. "I'll get some for all three of us."

"Thanks, Gavin," Adam muttered. He looked up nervously at the fire chief. What idea did he have?

"So I was thinking," Kurle said without further introduction. "This famous dog of yours..."

"Zeph, Sir."

"Zeph. That's right. This famous Zeph. I was thinking, maybe we could have him come to one of these dinners. We could have people take their picture next to Zeph, the amazing canine detective—for a small donation. All money would go to the fire company, of course. And maybe—well, you being a hero and all—maybe you could be in the pictures, too. Wouldn't that be cool? To have your picture taken with a local hero and his dog?"

Adam licked his lips, trying to think of what to say. "I didn't do anything that special. I just thought—"

"Oh, don't be modest, Adam. I read the article. I heard the stories. You were worried about your mother's special necklace, and you used your brain to find it. Though I'd love it if you became a firefighter when you got older, I'm thinking maybe you should be a detective instead."

"I—I never gave much thought to what I want to be when I grow up."

"It's never too early to start thinking about it," Kurle said. "What do you think you'd like to be?"

Adam shrugged, thinking about his parents. "I just want to be happy."

Kurle smiled. "That's the best answer I've ever heard to that question. The key is, you have to figure out what makes you happy. You could really go places in life, Adam."

Gavin returned with forks, knives, spoons, and butter. Kurle smiled. "We'll start small. What do you say about having Zeph here for a photo opportunity?"

Gavin's eyes widened. "That'd be so cool. You should do it during a crab feed, since those are the most popular events."

"That's a great idea, Gavin. And what a clever mind. Someone as clever as you should think about—oh, I don't know. Maybe going into business. Do you think you'd like running your own business?" He looked at the table full of food. "What about a restaurant?"

Gavin's smile faded. "My parents opened one, and it's not as easy as it seems."

Kurle patted Gavin on the back. "Things get easier with experience. You know, you have some great ideas, Gavin. Have you ever tried to help your parents think of ideas for their restaurant?"

Gavin shook his head.

"Maybe you should. You've got a clever head on those shoulders. Maybe you should think about ways to help your parents' business. You seem to have a talent for marketing."

"Marketing?"

Kurle nodded. "Yes. You know, advertising and promoting—getting people interested in supporting a business. You seem to have a talent for it."

Gavin smiled again. "I never thought of it that way. You're right. Maybe I could help them out."

Adam nodded, happy that the conversation no longer focused on him. He picked up a fork and dug into the spaghetti. It tasted delicious. Food always tasted best after hard work. Adam learned that during baseball season.

Kurle took a bite of a buttered roll and turned to Adam. "So what do you say? Can we count on you and Zeph to help us out with a fundraiser?"

Adam nodded. "Happy to help. And Zeph, too."

Kurle smiled and turned to Gavin. "And I trust I can count on you to help think of ways to promote this event and make it even better?"

"You bet!"

"We better finish eating," Adam said. "Sounds like the diners are getting loud again, which means they're probably done with their food, which means..."

"...the trash cans are probably getting full," Gavin said.

"Spencer will be upset if we let the trash cans overflow."

Kurle nodded. "He runs a tight ship, don't he? It's hard to find a good volunteer like him." Kurle smiled at the boys. "But I think I may have found two tonight."

Adam's ears burned even hotter as he and Gavin finished first their dinners and then their first night of volunteering.

~ Eight ~

Courtney checked her phone. Still no texts. It was already evening: the movie her friends saw was surely over by now, but they still hadn't texted her. She sat at the kitchen table and sighed. Even if they did text her, what did she have to say to them? Sapphie sat at her feet, staring up at her and cocking her head.

"Want to play fetch, Sapphie?"

Sapphie jumped like a baby kangaroo, and Courtney picked up her pink rabbit squeaky toy and threw it across the kitchen. Sapphie ran after it, her nails skittering on the floor. She dropped the toy and jumped again. Courtney threw it. She was glad for the noisy dog. Aside from Sapphie, the house was too quiet. Mom was upstairs editing. Dad had brought Adam to the fire hall, and he was probably out in his office. Zeph was probably with him, too. Because Zeph was quiet and well-behaved, Dad sometimes let Zeph nap in his office while he worked—if Adam wasn't home, of course.

Adam wouldn't be back until later. It was weird how she missed him. Courtney would even be glad to hear Adam reading his comic books to Zeph, or talking to his friends on the phone. The house was too quiet. Courtney had to get away.

"Mom!" Courtney called up the stairs. "I'm going outside to talk to Cassie."

"Okay," came the reply from the office.

"Come on, Sapphie. Let's get your leash."

Sapphie jumped and fidgeted while Courtney tried to attach her leash, but Courtney remembered the training. She took a deep breath, held out a hand, and very calmly said, "Sit."

Sapphie barked.

"No," Courtney said. "Sit."

Sapphie cried a moment longer but then sat. Her eyes were wide, though, as if she were obeying reluctantly.

"Better." Courtney attached the leash to Sapphie's collar. "Let's go."

Sapphie pulled down the street, huffing and choking.

"I'm going to have to put your harness on if you don't calm down," Courtney whined.

Sapphie continued toward the cul-de-sac. Instead of turning up the hilly driveway to Cassie's house, Sapphie pulled toward the woods, whining and barking quietly.

"No, Sapphie. We're going to visit Cassie."

Sapphie planted herself on the ground and barked.

"No."

Bark.

"No!"

Bark.

Courtney held up her hand the way the trainer taught her to, but Sapphie remained stubborn. Courtney dropped her hand. "Please, Sapphie. We can't go into the woods. There are ticks and snakes and all sorts of creepy things. Besides, it's getting dark. If there were any creepy crawlies, we'd never see them in all the shadow. Raccoons, deer, squirrels, cats..."

Sapphie's eyes popped open, and she jumped at her leash, biting and squealing. Courtney sighed again and picked up the squirming puppy, carrying her up the hill. She didn't even have to ring the doorbell. Cassie was already standing there, holding the door open for her.

"You must have heard Sapphie," Courtney said, entering Cassie's house.

"It's a little hard not to." Cassie looked down at the puppy wiggling in Courtney's arms. "What's gotten into her, anyway?"

"I don't know. She keeps wanting to pull into the woods."

"Here, I'll close the door so you can put her down."

Sapphie leapt from Courtney's arms and pounced at

the door just as it closed. Then she barked at it. When that didn't work, she stuck her nose under the door as far as it would go. She sniffed and sniffed and she jumped at the door one more time before lying down near it, whining.

"Just leave her," Cassie said. "Whatever it is will work itself out. Now as for you, how is everything going?"

"Okay." Courtney sighed.

Cassie frowned. "Just okay?"

Courtney nodded.

"How about some hot chocolate?"

Courtney unclipped Sapphie's leash and followed Cassie into the kitchen. Cassie put on some water to boil then winked at Courtney. She took a bag of pretzels and crinkled it. Immediately, a jingling collar could be heard in the foyer. Cassie crinkled the bag again. The collar jingled again. Then Cassie took out a pretzel and snapped it in half. Faster than a flash, Sapphie leapt up the steps and sat at Cassie's feet with the perfect posture for begging.

"I guess the way to Sapphie's heart really is through food." Courtney shrugged as Cassie fed the puppy some pretzels. "You should have seen her at the nursing home earlier today. There was this old guy there, and he fed her, like, his entire meal. She has never been happier."

"Sounds like maybe you had a little fun at the nursing home?"

Courtney shrugged. "There was this old guy, Mister Grindle. He doesn't like to follow the rules at all. He and his wife were talking to me a little bit, but mostly they just let me talk. Maybe next time he can tell me some more stories. It made me think maybe I'm not the only one who breaks the rules."

"But you're getting better about that, right?" Cassie mixed some chocolate powder into the boiling water. "I mean, you're trying not to break so many rules?"

Courtney nodded. "I'm trying."

"Which is why I'm so glad you're going to audition for the play. It's good to keep active. Involved." Cassie laughed warm-heartedly. "Hang out with friends who are good influences."

Courtney put her hand on the phone-shaped bulge in her pocket and wondered about her own friends. She took a seat at the kitchen table. "That's what I wanted to ask you about—getting involved in the play. I was hoping you could tell me a little bit about it."

Cassie hurried downstairs and returned a moment later with a thick packet of papers. She dropped it on the table in front of Courtney and then returned to the stove to stir the hot chocolate. Courtney looked down at the paper. It read:

Mister Baxter's Bookish Mess

"This is the script!" Courtney flipped to the first page.

"Sure is. You can read it if you want. Take it home. Bring it to auditions on Monday. I have lots of copies."

"Do I have to memorize anything for auditions?"

"No. You'll be able to read from the paper. We'll also do some improv to get a better idea of everyone's personalities."

"Improv?"

"It's short for 'improvisation.' It's when you act on the spot. If I told you right now to pretend you were a customer in a café in Paris, for example, you would have to make up words and facial gestures to go along with it."

"Sounds kind of like a game."

"Sort of. It's as fun as a game. Fun to watch, too." Cassie winked. "Want to try?"

"Try?"

"Some improv. Right now. Pretend you're at a café in Paris."

Courtney giggled. "Miss, I would like a croissant, see voo plate."

Cassie smiled. "It's '*s'il vous plait*,'" she whispered.

Courtney shrugged. "I don't know how to speak French."

Cassie nodded. "Just go with it. You're doing a good job."

Courtney sat up straighter. "Uno croissant, *s'il vous plait*," she said in her best French accent.

Cassie laughed. "Okay, maybe just a little more practice, but you get the idea."

Courtney turned back to the script. "So what's this play about? A bookstore, right?"

Cassie poured the hot chocolate into two mugs, added milk and whipped cream, and set the mugs on the kitchen table. "It's a fun play because there are so many characters. Many of the roles are small, so we can involve as many students as possible. The role I want you to audition for is the owner of a dog. You and the dog are both daredevils, and you were trying to pull off a dangerous trick—"

"What sort of trick?"

"The character you would be playing—Daring Dan, though if you get the role, we'll change the name to Daring Dani—has taught her dog—Denby Dog—how to skateboard. Before the play starts, both Dani and Denby get injured trying to perform a double-skateboard trick off a ramp. Dan—or Dani—breaks her leg. Denby breaks both of his when they get crushed under a skateboard."

Courtney cringed.

"During the play, Dani walks on crutches, and Denby uses a special cart made just for dogs so he can walk with only his front legs, pulling his back legs along and keeping them still so they can heal."

"So if I get the part, I'd have to walk on crutches." Courtney sipped her cocoa.

"That's right. I already contacted your school. The nurse has a pair we can borrow. I also contacted a dog rehabilitation company. They agreed to loan us a special cart for a dog to use during the play. We'll be donating proceeds from the play to research organizations that help dogs with spinal injuries and conditions that affect their ability to move around."

"So the dog in the play would be…Sapphie?"

Cassie raised an eyebrow. "If you think she's ready."

Courtney and Cassie turned to Sapphie. She was sitting under the kitchen table, her nose sniffing for more pretzels.

"What do you think, Sapphie? Can you handle being in a play? Are you far enough into your training?"

Sapphie whined.

"What do you think, Courtney?"

Courtney frowned. "She's getting better, but she listens to the instructor at obedience class much better than she listens to me. It's like she doesn't respect me or something. Maybe you should get my instructor to play the part of Daring Dan. She would listen to him for sure."

"Have you tried being firm with her?"

"That's what the teacher says to do. I guess I'm putting off vibes or something like that." Courtney looked down at her pocket and couldn't help but notice her cell phone hadn't vibrated even a single time. No one had texted her since earlier that afternoon. "Sometimes I wonder how I manage to mess everything up. I always seem to make my parents mad, I can never do as good in school as Adam, and since Halloween, I'm not even sure if I have friends anymore. Or who my friends are. Or why," she added in a whisper.

Cassie put a hand on Courtney's arm. "We all go through times like this. We question who we are, who our friends are, why we do the things we do. Growing up is tough. But we learn from everything we do—whether it was the best thing we ever did, or the worst."

Courtney sipped her cocoa again, staring out the kitchen window. Sapphie barked under the table. Courtney snapped out of her dream. "Sapphie, no."

Cassie smiled. "That sounded pretty confident, Courtney. Did you see how Sapphie quieted right away?"

"Yes."

"Keep up that level of confidence. With dog training, yes, but with life, too. Stay confident. Know what you want, and make sure all your actions correspond to what you want. Don't let other people make decisions for you. Don't do things because you think other people want you to. Do things because you know they're the right things to do. Understand what I'm saying?"

Courtney looked down at Sapphie, who had quieted and was sitting attentively, looking at Courtney as if awaiting a command. "I think so." Courtney smiled. She turned back to Cassie. "So tell me about some of these other characters in the play."

~ * ~

When Adam returned from his night at the fire hall, Courtney was curled up on the couch with Sapphie and Zeph at her feet. Mom was seated on the couch, reviewing some editing.

"How did it go, Adam?" Mom asked.

"Great!"

Zeph jumped up to greet him.

"Chief Kurle said Adam and Gavin did really well," Dad added.

"Good to hear." Mom put down her editing. "When will you be volunteering again? I need to make sure we keep our appointments straight on the family calendar. Now that you and Courtney are so busy, we have to make sure we write everything down accurately."

"I'll make sure to write it down good," Adam said, winking.

Mom's eyes flashed. "You mean *well.*"

"Write it down *well,*" Adam corrected. He checked his notebook. "I'm volunteering each Saturday night for the next few weeks. November twenty-second is Bingo Night. No, the twenty-third. The Saturday after that, the fire hall is closed for Thanksgiving."

"That's right," Mom said. "November twenty-seventh. Thanksgiving falls so late this year."

81

Adam nodded. "The Saturday after that is the big one. It's the crab feed. December seventh—I mean eighth. Fire Chief Kurle asked if I would bring Zeph. He heard about our work this summer finding the burglar, and he wants Zeph to be available to take pictures with diners in exchange for donations to the fire hall."

"Adam is being modest," Dad said. "Fire Chief Kurle said Adam gets to be in the pictures, too."

Adam felt his ears burning red, so he turned to Zeph instead. "Zeph, would you like to be in pictures?"

Zeph's ears perked up. "Arooo!" he howled.

Courtney cleared her throat. "That's the same weekend as my play," she said.

"What play?"

"I'm going to be in a play called *Mister Baxter's Bookish Mess*. We're having auditions next week, and we rehearse four times a week between now and the beginning of December. We perform Saturday night and Sunday at two o'clock. There's even a dog character, and Cassie says Sapphie gets to play it. The dog's name is Denby, and—"

Adam raised an eyebrow.

Dad cleared his throat. "Is Sapphie good enough to play a role in a play? Will she listen?"

Mom nodded. "She's been getting much better since these obedience classes have started. I think she can handle it. Courtney, you'll show her the way."

Courtney smiled.

"The beginning of December seems so close. How are you going to put together a play that quick?" Dad scratched his head.

"Quickly." Mom smiled. "Cassie's in charge. It's a program she puts on for middle-school students. It helps them intensely focus." She winked at Dad. Adam smiled. Intensely focusing on something wholesome would be good for Courtney.

Dad nodded. "So many events coming up. We'll have to plan on seeing the show opening night, Courtney.

Although, if we did that, we'd miss seeing Adam be the star of the night during the crab feed. Maybe, Susan, you could go to Courtney's show opening night, and I could go to the crab feed—and then I'd go to Courtney's show for the Sunday matinee. What do you think?"

"I want to see her show, too," Adam said. He couldn't picture Courtney acting on stage. Whether she did well or bombed, Adam wanted to be there to see her. He chuckled. *Especially* if she bombed.

"That could work." Mom bit her lip. "On your way up to bed, everyone should write down schedules on the family calendar in the kitchen. Otherwise, we'll get all mixed up."

"Speaking of getting mixed up," Adam asked. "I meant to ask you if I could have a sleepover with Gavin and Patrick sometime soon. Like maybe Friday?"

Courtney snarled. "That's not fair. I'm not allowed to have a sleepover."

Mom stood up and crossed her arms. "You've been very good today, Courtney. This was your first outburst, so I'm going to try to stay calm. But do you remember when you had that sleepover at the end of the summer? Remember what the three of you did to Adam's backpack? And I don't have to remind you about what happened at Halloween." She took a deep breath. "You've been doing well turning over a new leaf, but you have to remember that no one changes overnight, and trust has to be earned back gradually. When you are ready—and only then—you'll be allowed to have another sleepover. Between now and then, you focus on getting that dog of yours fully trained, staying involved in as many activities as possible, and keeping out of trouble."

She turned to Adam. "As for you, Adam, I'm glad to see you making new friends. You boys can have a sleepover on Friday. I'll give Patrick and Gavin's parents a call. But I will give you the same warning I gave Courtney. You have our trust until you choose to break it, so make sure you and your friends make smart decisions, too."

"I will," Adam said. He avoided eye contact with his sister. He could tell she was mad at him.

"Courtney?" Mom asked. "Do you understand what I've said?"

Courtney's anger broke into understanding, and Adam let out a sigh of relief. Lately, she seemed like she was genuinely trying to change. Adam smiled at her.

"I do, Mom. For now I'm focusing on training Sapphie and staying out of trouble." She turned to Sapphie. "Looks like you and Zeph are *both* going to be stars."

~ Nine ~

That night, everyone was too distracted to give Sapphie her usual amount of pre-bedtime attention. She huffed into her crate and whined. The nerve of some people!

"Mark down a matinee on the eighth of December," Courtney was saying.

"What's a matinee?" Adam asked. "How do you spell it?"

"Pay attention to me," Sapphie barked.

"Quiet, Sapphie," Courtney said. She turned back to Adam. "Here, give me the pen. A matinee is a two o'clock show. And mark down opening night. The seventh of December."

"And the date of the sleepover," Person Mom called from upstairs. "I don't want to get confused."

"And all the dates you're volunteering at the fire house," Person Dad called from upstairs.

"Me, me, *me*!" Sapphie barked. Why did people always talk about silly things?

Adam grabbed the pen from Courtney.

"Hush, Sapphie!" Courtney turned back to Adam. "Give me the pen again. I need to fill in all the dates I'm volunteering at the nursing home," added Courtney, snatching the pen back.

"And the night of the eighth is my crab feed," said Adam. "Six o'clock."

Courtney and Adam were fighting over a pen and writing something on the wall. So boring. If only she could get a hold of that pen, she could chew it to pieces. It probably tasted great, too! But she was stuck in her crate, and Zeph said she shouldn't try to escape in front of People. Sapphie turned around three times and tried to get comfortable. Courtney was supposed to give her a treat, wasn't she? Then she and Adam would go upstairs. Sapphie couldn't wait. She had so much to discuss with Zeph.

Finally, after much nonsense and pointless discussion with Adam, Courtney turned to the dogs. "Alright, Sapphie, time for bed. Here's a treat! You get one, too, Zeph."

Both dogs snapped to attention as something delicious wafted through the air. Their noses twitched, and neither could help the drool dripping from their mouths. It wasn't dainty, but it was necessary.

"Bacon strips!" Sapphie barked.

"I can't wait to try it," barked Zeph.

"Okay, but quiet, you guys." Courtney waited until they quieted. Then she handed each one a bacon strip through the crate doors.

"Goodnight, Zeph," Adam said. "Night, Sapphie."

Courtney turned out the light, and Sapphie waited to hear the two people walk upstairs. She could hear Zeph devouring his bacon strip in his crate. She wanted very much to eat hers, but a single word echoed in her mind: Shadow. So she hid it under her cushion and buried it with her blanket.

"That was delicious!" Zeph said. "Where did Courtney get those?"

Sapphie sat on top of her buried treat and hoped her brother couldn't smell it. "She got them from Sir."

"Wow, I like this 'Sir' Person even more!"

"He's sneaky, Zeph. He's far too sneaky." Sapphie could still hear Zeph licking his lips.

"Maybe one day I'll get to meet him. It sounds like I'm going to meet someone else, though."

"Who?"

"Fire Chief Kurle."

"Who's that?"

"I don't know, but Adam was telling me we're going to go see him together, and people are going to take pictures of me."

"Why?"

"It's going to help the fire company."

"What's a fire company, Zeph?"

"I'm not sure. It might be a company that makes fires."

"What would they do that for?"

"Well, when our people cook food, they need to heat it somehow. Maybe they buy each heat from the fire company."

"You're smart, Zeph." Sapphie licked her paw. "But that sounds like a boring thing to make. You know what would be more fun to make?"

"What?"

"Bacon strips, bacon strips, *bacon strips*!"

A weary voice shouted from upstairs: "Sapphie, be quiet. It's time to sleep."

"Hmph! Do you hear that? The nerve. That's no way to talk to a star."

"A star?"

"That's right. Not only am I a princess. I'm going to be a star, too."

"What do you mean?"

"I was over at Cassie's house with Courtney today."

"And?"

"They were telling me about a thing I'm going to be in. It's called a 'play.' Have you ever heard of a play, Zeph?"

"Yes."

Zeph heard of practically every word ever made. How annoying. "Well, anyway. I'm going to be in a play. Courtney is going to be someone named Dan Daring Daredevil or something, and I'm going to be someone named Denby Dog. I have to practice with this thing called a cart, and Courtney has to practice with this thing called a crutches. We both get to be stars in the play. People get to watch us and love us. If we do good, we get lots of treats."

Sapphie was speaking so quickly that she started panting. "There's so many different characters in the play, and they all get to talk to me 'cause I'm the cutest one in the play. There's Dan Daredevil, of course, and then there's Mrs. Morris, who is looking for a scary story. See, it takes place at a bookstore. What's a bookstore, Zeph? And then there's a boy named Jack who's looking for a book for a book report. What's that, Zeph? And then a girl named Sally who's looking for candy—I know what *that* is—and it turns out she's in the wrong store, but Mister Baxter has some candy anyway. See, Mister Baxter is the owner of the bookstore, and he's a character, too, and then—"

"Sapphie, calm down!" Zeph barked.

"But, but—"

"First of all, a bookstore is a place to buy books."

"What are they?"

"You know those things our people are always looking at?"

"You mean the sparkly toy Courtney always used to have? She looked at it all the time."

"Not that one. I'm talking about the thing Person Mom always has."

"Oooh. Books. Those are boring, boring, *boring*! Unless you get to chew on one. Remember that time we chewed on Adam's comic book? It was so crispy, and I loved the ripping sound it made as we tore it apart. It was fun, fun, *fun*!"

"Sapphie, calm down. We got in big trouble for chewing up that book. Besides, that isn't the point of books. I don't think you understand what the play is about."

"Of course I do! It's about how cute I am, and how all the people in the play love me, even though I'm stuck in a wheely cart. What do you think of that, Zeph?"

Zeph cocked his head under the moonlight. "Sounds like a lot of hard work. You don't understand what you're getting into. Are you ready to work hard?"

"Hmph!" Sapphie bit one of the bars of her crate. "I don't have to work hard. I'm so cute, I can do anything I please. Everyone will love me no matter what. I'm going to be the best actress ever. I'll be famous, and everyone who sees me will bring me bacon and peanut butter treats."

"If you're in a play, everyone is going to act like Sir. They're going to tell you what to do."

Sapphie yelped. "No! Everyone is going to watch me and applaud, and treat me like a princess."

Zeph growled. "You're not listening, Sapphie."

"You're wrong, wrong, *wrong*!" Sapphie bit her crate again. "Being an actress is nothing like you think. I will be able to do whatever I want. Shadow would understand. Hmph!"

"Suit yourself." Zeph turned around three times. Sapphie could hear him snuggling into his comforter. "But after your first rehearsal, you're going to see what I mean. You're going to be told what to do all the time. You're not going to like it at all."

"We'll see, Zeph."

"We *will* see, Sapphie. I am glad of one thing."

"What's that?"

"When you're in the play with Courtney, you won't be here, so you can't escape and run off into the woods again."

Sapphie stood stone still. "Wait, what?"

"You'll be so busy with rehearsal, and People will be watching you all the time. You won't be able to run off any more."

"What?"

Zeph's breathing became steady with sleep, and Sapphie sat alone in the moonlight. Was Zeph right? If she joined Courtney in Mister Baxter's play, would she have to give up her time with Shadow? What if she couldn't escape anymore? What if People watched her all the time and told her what to do? What if this play took away all her freedom? What if everyone *was* like Sir? What would happen to her Shadow? Who would help feed him? Maybe being a star wasn't as good as she thought.

She plopped down into her comforter and smelled the delicious scent of bacon. She could hardly wait for Shadow to have some. But first, she'd have to think of a solution to her problem. She had to find a way out of the play. Courtney said she'd get to be in the play if she was a good dog. So, naturally, she had to find a way to be bad.

~ Ten ~

On the afternoon of November seventeenth, Courtney trudged into the auditorium of Red Rose Middle School. Her feet clip-clopped against the old linoleum floor as she made her way down the center aisle to the stage. There, Cassie and two other grown-ups stood pointing and talking.

Cassie held a clipboard and marked things down every now and then. One of the other grown-ups, a young man about Cassie's age, was arranging students in lines. The third adult, a woman older than Cassie, was busy handing out sheets of paper to the students as they lined up. Courtney stared at the others waiting to audition. Some of them were stretching. Others mouthed words from their papers. Still others bounced up and down. Courtney had never acted before—not unless lying counted—and had no idea what to do. She looked down at her hand to see that she was shaking.

"Courtney!" Cassie waved. "Come this way."

Cassie marked something on her clipboard. The young man, who wore a name tag that said "Marty," directed Courtney to stand at the end of the line. Cassie whispered something to the other woman, whose name tag read "Gloria," and Gloria handed Courtney a sheet of paper. It was a single page out of the script. Courtney recognized it. After Cassie loaned her the script, Courtney read it twice. Hers was the part of Daring Dan, or in this case, Daring Dani. Courtney almost knew the lines by heart.

Still, she couldn't shake her nerves. Her heart pounded, and her mouth went dry. She wished she still had her cell phone. Mom promised to bring Sapphie to the auditions, and if she had her cell phone, Courtney could have texted and asked for a bottle of water.

"Live and learn," Courtney whispered. Maybe if she continued behaving, she'd get her cell phone back sooner rather than later.

"Alright, everyone!" Gloria called. "Time to get started."

Courtney looked around. No one looked as nervous as she felt. She tried to focus on the woman in front of her, and she grasped her paper tightly to keep from shaking.

"My name is Gloria, and these are my colleagues, Cassie and Marty. We're here with Transitions, a program to expose young people to the power of theatre. I'm delighted to see such a turnout! Unfortunately, there are more people here to audition than there are parts in the play."

The room filled with groans.

"However, we don't like to turn anyone away, so anyone who doesn't get a part will still be invited to help. There are many ways you can help with a play besides being on stage as an actor. We need help with set construction, sound or lighting, or even designing the programs. So everyone, stay confident and happy. It'll help with your audition. Nerves are only useful in small amounts."

Courtney tried to swallow with her dry tongue and wished her nerves were only there in a small amount.

"First of all, everyone needs to understand that we have a rigorous rehearsal schedule, practicing every week on Monday, Tuesday, Wednesday, and Thursday. We won't practice the Wednesday before Thanksgiving, or Thanksgiving itself, and we'll perform twice for the community, December seventh, a Saturday evening, and December eighth, a Sunday matinee. Your principal has also asked for us to perform the play for the school one day during the week of December ninth. If you cannot attend the rehearsals and performances, I'll have to ask you to leave now. We can only accept students willing to work hard for the next three weeks. It's an intense program. We only take the most dedicated. Think carefully about whether you can make the commitment."

The room silenced. A few students stepped out of line and walked up the aisle, their feet clip-clopping on the linoleum floor until they exited the auditorium. Courtney felt her face flush. She didn't mind making the commitment, but she worried about one thing Gloria said. If she got a part, she would be asked to perform for the whole school during the school day. Aileen would be there to see it. So would Meghan and Noelle. They would have their cell phones, too, and they'd probably record the whole thing— or at least the parts Courtney was in. They'd be sure to record anything embarrassing and post it online. After all, Courtney used to do the same thing when she hung out with them. It didn't feel so nice being on the other end.

Courtney took a deep breath.

Gloria turned back to the remaining students. "Very good, then. You who are still here have already taken the first step to greatness. You are dedicated. You have confidence that, given the next three weeks, you'll be able to pull together a fabulous play." She applauded them. "We've given each of you a part to read. It's one we think you'll be good at based on your appearance and stature. We'll choose the best for each role. If it seems you're not right for the part you're reading, we might give you a different part."

Marty stepped up beside Gloria. "But first, we want you to warm up. We want to see you at your most natural. We want all those nerves to disappear. We're going to do— a little improv. Does anyone know what that is?"

The room fell silent. Wary eyes looked around. Cassie cleared her throat and looked at Courtney. Courtney hated being called on in school. She hardly ever knew the answer, so it was easier not to pay attention. But this time, she knew the right answer, and Cassie knew that she knew. Reluctantly, Courtney put her hand up.

"Yes?" Marty called.

"Improv is a type of acting where people—" Courtney scratched her chin. "Where people make things up on the spot instead of memorizing lines."

"Very good," Marty said. "And your name is?"

"Courtney. Courtney Hollinger."

"Very good, Courtney. I'd like to invite you to be first. Come on up to the stage. Everyone, let's give her a round of applause."

The auditorium clapped as Courtney walked up the steps to the stage. They were hollow and wooden, and it felt like her footsteps echoed through the entire school. She stood on the stage and tried to swallow, but her tongue was still dry. Where was Mom with Sapphie? She usually had a bottle of water in her purse.

"Now Courtney, we're going to take ideas from the audience to start a scene. But first, let's choose a partner for you." Marty pointed to a boy in a hockey jersey. Courtney recognized him but didn't know his name. He was president of the French Club and always hung out in the library during lunch. He was probably more of a dork than Adam!

"I'm Sean," he said.

Marty clapped his hands. "Alright, let's give Sean and Courtney another round of applause."

Courtney felt her face flush again. She had never been on stage before, and she'd never been the center of attention, either—at least, not in a good way. It was a strange feeling, and it made her heart race.

"Now we'll take suggestions from the audience. Give our actors a situation. What are they doing? Where are they?"

"A hockey game!" someone shouted.

"Okay." Marty turned to Courtney. "You two are at a hockey game. Go!"

Courtney's head spun. Go? What was she supposed to do? Go where? Do what? Sean seemed to be more aware of the rules.

Sean leaned over and held his hands downward as if

94

he were holding a hockey stick. "I told you," he screamed. "No spectators on the ice! Go back to your seat, ma'am."

"What?" Courtney squealed.

"Play along," Marty said, waving his hand in encouragement. "You're a spectator that made her way onto the ice during—"

"During the regional semi-finals," Sean said. "And you're causing a distraction."

"What?" Courtney looked around. The spectators blurred into a wall around her.

"Play along," Cassie whispered from the auditorium.

"Okay. I, um, didn't mean to come out onto the ice. I was, um..."

"You were what, ma'am? I'm going to have to call security to escort you—" Sean leaned over to grab Courtney's arm, and Courtney threw her hand up in the air to stop him.

"Freeze!" Marty called.

Both Sean and Courtney froze where they were. "Alright, I need two more actors to take their places. Stand exactly in the positions they're standing in." Marty chose two new actors from the line. They came onto the stage and stood in the exact same positions Courtney and Sean were standing in.

"I need a new scenario," Marty said. "Call something out, quick!"

"The cafeteria!" someone called.

"Great!" Marty clapped his hands. "Courtney, Sean, you two may re-join the audience. The two actors on stage, start your scene in a cafeteria. And...go!"

The person who took Courtney's spot was Henry, a student in Courtney's English class. The one who took Sean's spot was Derrick, a class clown. Derrick held Henry's arm the same way Sean held Courtney's.

"Oh no you don't!" Derrick shouted. "That's the last time you throw a pudding cup in my face. I'm calling the principal on you. Who do you think you are?"

Henry picked up on it right away, and he took his hand—the one that Courtney had left sticking up in the air—and made a flinging motion with it. "There!" Henry shouted. "I just flung even more pudding at you, and I'll do it again, too. What are you going to do about it?"

"Freeze and switch!" Marty clapped his hands, and two more students took the stage, starting in the positions in which Henry and Derrick had frozen. Courtney was starting to get it. "I need a new scenario."

"They're lost," Courtney shouted. "And their GPS is broken." She smiled, thinking of her mother.

Marty nodded. "Excellent suggestion. You are lost, and your GPS is broken. And...go!"

Courtney smiled as she watched the next pair of actors, anxious to take her next turn at improv. Some of the actors were funny, some were serious, others were sad, and some couldn't stop smiling. Courtney realized how bland her own performance had been. She decided when her turn came up again, she would be as dramatic as possible. She couldn't wait to hear what her scenario would be.

Finally, it was her turn again. The actors before her had frozen in a chase scene. Cassie called them this time. "Courtney and Sean, you're up. Since you were first, we'll give you one more shot at it. Then we'll move on to the auditions. I need a scenario!"

Someone in the audience chuckled. "A hockey game!"

Cassie shrugged. "Okay, we'll end where we started: they're at a hockey game."

Sean took the place of the actor who was doing the chasing, and Courtney stood where the second actor was being chased.

"And...action!" Cassie shouted.

Immediately, Sean started chasing her around the stage. He swung an invisible hockey stick in the air and took long strides as if he were skating. "I told you, Miss. You must get off the ice!"

Courtney widened her eyes and frowned. She put a hand to her forehead and moaned. "Oh, but you don't understand! My poor little dog got loose, and I'm trying to catch her. Don't you see her?"

Sean stopped chasing and put a hand over his eyes, looking out over the audience. "I don't see this dog of yours, Miss. I'm afraid I'm going to have to call security. We've got a hockey game to play."

Just as he finished his line, the auditorium door opened, and Courtney's mother stepped inside, leading Sapphie on a leash.

Sean frowned. "Now that you mention it, Miss, I do think I see a dog. Maybe you're not so crazy after all."

"And, cut!" Marty shouted. "Great job, everyone. You really got the hang of improv by the end. Now hopefully you're all feeling warmed up, so we can start—"

But none of the actors were listening to Marty. Instead, they stared at Sapphie as she trotted down the aisle.

"Sorry I'm late," Mom said. "There was a car wash on the side of the road, and their signs were all wrong. I had to stop and help them with their spelling. Can you believe it? They spelled 'Get your car cleaned' as C-L-E-E-N-D."

Courtney shook her head.

"The man behind the counter wouldn't believe me, either."

Cassie smiled. "That's okay, Mrs. Hollinger. You're just in time. We're about to start auditions. In fact, let's have Sapphie go first. That way, we can see how she does when there are other distractions around."

She went backstage and brought out a small red cart with two large rubber wheels on the back.

"What is that?" asked Kevin, a boy who had pretended to be the abominable snowman in his skit.

Cassie sat at the edge of the stage with the cart. "This is a canine mobility cart. We borrowed it for the purpose of this play. In the play, there is a daredevil dog and her owner. Both the dog, Denby, and the owner have broken their legs trying to perform a dangerous trick. This cart is like a wheelchair for dogs. These types of carts are used to help dogs with conditions that affect their movement. It allows the dog to pull herself forward with her front legs, in this case, allowing the back legs to heal. Courtney has kindly allowed her dog, Sapphie, to audition for this role. I borrowed a cart that would be roughly Sapphie's size."

"Can we see it?" asked Marie, the girl who during improv pretended to be a scarecrow that came to life.

Cassie motioned everyone over, including Sapphie and Mrs. Hollinger. She pointed out the various features of the cart, including an explanation of how Sapphie would be strapped inside. Courtney felt her skin prickling. She couldn't imagine Sapphie staying still long enough to be put in a cart. And what if Sapphie didn't listen? She could wheel herself right off the stage. Then she'd hurt herself for real. Courtney swallowed a lump in her throat and wondered whether this was really such a good idea. Mom was holding Sapphie now, and the dog's eyes looked wild and wide. Her nose twitched as her head snapped from one direction to the other. She panted hard with excitement, and her legs wouldn't stop wiggling.

Courtney even wondered whether it would be better if Sapphie didn't get the part at all. It would be so much work trying to keep the wild little dog under control—all that on top of learning her own lines and learning how to walk on crutches. For a moment, Courtney wondered if the well-behaved Zeph might be a better choice.

It was almost as if Mom had read her thoughts. "Here." She handed Sapphie over to Courtney. "She's your dog. You have to be the one she listens to. Learn to control her. Stay relaxed. Calm. But in control."

Courtney took the squirming puppy and nodded. Then she watched her mother walk into the auditorium and choose a seat in the middle row.

Cassie was still speaking. "...and very important for dogs who not only get injured, but who develop spinal conditions—like *degenerative myelopathy*—that limit their ability to move on their own. That's why part of our proceeds from this play will be donated to an organization that helps such animals." She turned to Sapphie. "Ready to try it out, cutie?"

Sapphie barked.

The actors cleared the way so that Courtney and Sapphie could get through. Courtney put the wiggling dog down on the stage, next to the rolling cart.

"We should take off her leash," Cassie said. "So she doesn't get tangled."

Courtney tried to swallow. "Are you sure that's a good idea?"

"I've seen her interacting with you lately. She's becoming a good dog. She's doing really well with those classes. I think you should trust her more."

"If you say so." Courtney unclipped the leash. Sapphie leapt into the air and barked. She ran to the edge of the stage, sniffing and licking each of the actors. They seemed delighted to greet her, showering her with praise and compliments:

"Good dog!"

"What a cute girl!"

"She's a little princess!"

Courtney could tell Sapphie adored the attention. She rolled over and allowed her belly to be rubbed. When Courtney approached to pick her up again, however, Sapphie snapped to her feet and barked. She ran in circles around Courtney. She widened the circle each time she ran so that soon she was running all around the stage.

Courtney breathed hard. Her heart pounded in her ears, and she felt her face becoming red and sweaty. "Sapphie, please stop!" She dashed around actors and leapt over chairs, chasing the tiny dog. She wondered how fast the story of Courtney and her badly-behaved dog would travel through the school. It wasn't exactly a "cool" thing to be known for. She hoped it didn't hurt her reputation too badly. "Sapphie!"

"She'll tire herself out," Cassie said. She tapped the stage. "Sapphie, come here, girl."

Sapphie answered with a bark before disappearing into the curtains back stage.

"Oh great!" Courtney ran after the dog. "You're in big trouble, Sapphie!" Courtney's voice echoed through the auditorium as she chased Sapphie backstage.

"Well, everyone, let's start the reading portion of the auditions. Courtney will audition when she gets back with Sapphie. Alright, then. Who's first?"

Courtney could just make out the beginning of the first audition as she hurried through the shadowy maze of the areas backstage, following the sound of clicking claws and panting breath.

~ Eleven ~

Sapphie navigated the shadows and curtains back stage like an expert. It was much easier to run through the backstage of a school than through the tangled undergrowth of the woods. Courtney kept calling her, and each time she did, Sapphie wanted to run to her Person and behave. But she kept reminding herself: Shadow.

In fact, she smelled evidence of mice as she entered the building with Person Mom. There had to be mice around here somewhere. Shadow would enjoy that. Maybe she could find one or two.

"Sapphie, stop!" Courtney shouted.

Sapphie fought the urge to listen. "Be bad," she reminded herself. "You need your days to be free for Shadow. You don't want to be a star."

"Sapphie, come on. You love attention! If you come back, you'll get to be a star in the show."

"Be bad, bad, *bad*!" Sapphie told herself. What would a bad dog do?

She stopped short in front of Courtney and barked. "Bad, bad, *bad*!" Then she squatted and left a wet mess on the stage. She wagged her tail and barked again before running off.

"Mom!" Courtney yelled to the auditorium. "Sapphie peed backstage!"

Courtney's voice echoed again, and the auditorium filled with laughter, but Sapphie didn't stay long enough to hear it all. She behaved badly enough for now, causing enough of a distraction to search for the mice. She smelled them back toward the exit.

She found a heating vent in the wall—slotted metal that allowed the mice to squeeze inside. She could see them cowering in the corner behind the grate, their eyes reflecting the red light of the sign above the door. Zeph would know what the sign said. Probably "Mice" or "Princess" or something like that. Sapphie didn't have time to learn about things like that. She had more important things to learn—things Shadow taught her.

Things like hunting.

She clawed at the grate, and it made a horribly loud echo. Courtney would be able to find her for sure. She had to hurry. She stood on her hind legs and pushed all her weight against the grate. It was old and rickety, and it started to give. "Break, break, *break*!" she barked.

"Sapphie, stop that immediately!" shouted a voice that was quickly approaching. It was Person Mom. That meant double trouble. Now Sapphie had two people after her. She pounced one last time at the ventilation cover, and just as she felt it give way, Person Mom reached out of nowhere and picked her up.

"No, no, *no*!" Sapphie shouted.

"Stop barking, Sapphie," Person Mom said. "You've been a very bad dog. I don't think you're cut out for acting in this play. And you embarrassed Courtney in front of her friends. You should see how upset she is. What a bad, bad dog."

Sapphie wagged her tail. After all, her goal was to be bad, so she actually did good, right? Person Mom didn't seem to think so. Person Mom carried Sapphie over to where Courtney was stooped over backstage, holding a paper towel roll and a spray bottle. Courtney's breathing sounded all weird, and she was doing that watery thing with her eyes—the thing Zeph warned her about.

Person Mom clipped the leash to Sapphie and put her on the floor next to Courtney. Courtney turned to her. Her face was red and streaked with water. She looked sad, like the time she got in trouble on Halloween.

"This is all your fault, Sapphie," Courtney cried.

Sapphie squealed and plopped down on the floor next to Courtney.

"Why do you have to be so bad all the time?"

Courtney asked.

At the word "bad," Sapphie barked.

"There's no way you can be in this play. I'll have to tell them all about this at obedience school on Friday."

Sapphie wasn't sure exactly what Courtney was saying, but she didn't like being the one responsible for Courtney's sadness.

"Maybe I'd better take her in the car," Person Mom said. "We'll wait for you out there. Try to calm down so you can audition. Then, I'll bet if you asked Adam, he'd let you borrow Zeph to be in the play. Zeph's a bit mellower than his sister. I bet he'd do a fabulous job. Sapphie can stay home with me in the afternoons. What do you say?"

Courtney nodded, and she tried to speak, but her breathing was all strange and uneven.

"Come on, Sapphie." Person Mom tugged on the leash. "Let's go in the car."

Sapphie's ears perked up at hearing one of her favorite activities. "In the car!" she barked. "Car, car, car!" See, maybe she *did* do good after all! Person Mom was rewarding her for her efforts. Even better, it sounded like she'd have her afternoons free. She could spend all her time with Shadow.

~ * ~

Even after Courtney finished cleaning up Sapphie's accident, she hid backstage. She didn't want to come out while the rest of the actors were still there. Not until she heard Miss Gloria say, "Okay, auditions are over! Results will be posted on the bulletin board outside this auditorium tomorrow morning. Be sure to check when you come to school. And if you didn't get a part, come to rehearsal tomorrow anyway. We'll have a backstage job for you all!"

Courtney snuck onto the stage. Cassie was picking up a few loose pieces of paper. Courtney cleared her throat.

"Sorry," she whispered.

Cassie frowned. "I guess little Sapphie isn't ready. Probably just too much excitement for her. She'll be ready one day."

"You still need a dog for the play, though."

"Yes, we do."

"My mom suggested that Zeph would be able to do it. He's perfect, just like my brother. He isn't trouble like Sapphie or me. He'll listen to whoever gets the part of Daring Dan. I'll look after him while I'm doing my work backstage. Maybe I can do sound. Or lighting."

"Are you saying you don't want to act anymore?"

Courtney tried to keep her breathing steady. It was still shaky from all the crying. "I missed auditions."

"No you didn't. We got to see you twice during the improv session, and I'm not sure if you realize it, but when you were dashing after Sapphie, you looked like quite the daredevil. And when you were shouting after Sapphie, we heard how loud you could be. I was talking to Gloria and Marty about it. You got the part."

"What?"

"Congratulations! You've got the part of Daring Dani, companion of Denby Dog, which will be played by Zeph."

"If Adam says it's okay."

Cassie smiled. "I'm sure he will."

"I'm sure he will, too."

~ Twelve ~

Afternoon was the best time to be alone. Person Mom was always busy finishing her editing (boring). Person Dad was always out in his office (boring). Adam was happy reading comic books or doing homework (boring). Starting today, Zeph would be going to play rehearsals with Cassie and Courtney. And that meant Sapphie was on her own.

Adam had let Sapphie into the backyard by herself. "You play," he told her. "I'll come get you in about ten minutes. I'm going to finish this math homework."

"Boring, boring, *boring*!" Sapphie barked.

"Be good," Adam said before closing the sliding glass door. In his hurry, he slammed it too hard, and it bounced open again. "Whoops," he said, and closed it more gently.

Sapphie wasn't sure how long ten minutes was, but she was certain it was enough time to escape, talk to Shadow, and return before getting caught. She spit out her bacon strip, the one she had kept buried in her crate. She had to think about how to escape, and keeping the treat in her mouth was too much of a temptation. She left it on the patio and trotted around the yard, looking for a way out. Each time she found a way out, her people found a way to keep her in.

First they filled in her adventure tunnel. It had taken her days and days to dig it out, but they filled it faster than she could bark. Then, they moved the patio furniture further from the fence so she couldn't use it as a springboard anymore. She was good at jumping, but they put a latch on the gate door that she couldn't figure out. A few days ago, though, she had discovered a loose slat in the fence, and that was going to be her way out. She checked to see if Adam was watching, but he was nowhere near the sliding glass door. Person Mom was nowhere to be found, either, and Sapphie could see Person Dad through the window of his office. He was speaking into that boxy toy—the one Courtney used to use all the time—so she knew he'd be too distracted to notice her.

She hurried back to the patio to retrieve her uneaten bacon strip, then trotted to the back of the yard and pushed the loose slat with her nose. She pushed her head through, eased her front paws out, and got stuck. She pulled and pulled—she was a growing puppy, after all, and getting bigger every day—until she finally got through. She'd have to find a better way to escape. She'd worry about that later, though. For now, she had to find Shadow.

She dashed into the woods beyond the cul-de-sac. She loved the way the crunchy leaves felt under her paws, and they hid so many smells that she could stay out there forever. She often thought about living there with Shadow but wondered if she would miss her People. She sniffed around some undergrowth.

"Shadow, is that you?"

The bush rattled, and something scampered through the leaves in the opposite direction. It was too small to be Shadow. In fact, it might have been a mouse, but Sapphie couldn't catch it with a bacon strip in her mouth.

Something else slithered in the undergrowth. It sounded like a snake—a big one. Sapphie only liked playing with the little ones. "Shadow?" Sapphie whimpered. "Where are you?"

From a tree branch came an echoing "Meow!"

"Shadow!" Sapphie ran to the tree, wagging her tail. She stood on her hind legs, clawing at the tree. "I missed you, Shadow! Come down and talk to me."

Shadow sat, perched. "Not yet."

Sapphie whimpered. "I wish I could climb trees, too! Will you teach me, Shadow?"

With another *meow*, the dark gray cat jumped from one of the branches to a lower one. The branch bounced up and down with his weight.

Sapphie sat. "You're getting bigger, too!" she

announced. "I almost couldn't fit through the fence today because I'm growing so fast—"

Shadow took another leap and landed with a soft thud in the leaves next to Sapphie.

Sapphie rubbed Shadow's neck with her nose. "I wish I could jump as good as you, Shadow! Maybe you can teach me."

Shadow licked his paw before he answered. "I told you already, Sapphie, dogs can't jump like cats can."

"What? But I am a cat, too. At least, sometimes I am. I'm a cat when I'm in the woods just like you."

Shadow continued licking his paw. "You've forgotten our discussion from last time, haven't you, silly dog?"

Sapphie wagged her tail. "You're a silly dog, too, Shadow."

"I'm not a dog, Sapphie."

"A cat, I mean. Because you live in the woods."

"Just because I live in the woods doesn't make me a—oh, nevermind. It's hopeless. Have you got something in your mouth, Sapphie? You're a little difficult to understand today."

"Oh!" Sapphie dropped the bacon strip. "I brought you a present. It's another bacon strip. You seemed to like it last time. And it's been sitting in my mouth for a while, so it's all mushy the way you like it."

Shadow bent down to inspect the bacon strip. Then he ate it—slowly and daintily.

"You eat slower than my brother, you know."

But Shadow didn't reply because he was too busy eating. Sapphie waited and watched. She loved watching Shadow eat. He was so different-looking than Zeph. His eyes were so piercing and bright. His paws were so quick and graceful. Sapphie hunched her back and tried to imitate the way he ate, using a dried leaf instead of a bacon strip, but she couldn't eat slowly at all. Before she realized it, she had eaten the whole leaf in one gulp.

"I've been practicing walking like you," Sapphie said

while Shadow finished the bacon. "Want to see?"

Sapphie walked slowly, with her legs out straight, lifting them high each time she stepped. She then arched her back and tried to *meow*, but it came out as a low *growl* instead.

Shadow looked up. "This meal was acceptable, Sapphie. Bring me more soon."

Sapphie wagged her tail. "I knew you'd like it. I was extra good at obedience class to earn that bacon strip, and I tried *real* hard not to eat it so you could have it instead! I will get you another bacon strip when I go back to see Sir."

"Very well." Shadow licked his paw again. "Now you will help me find a mouse to eat."

Sapphie wagged her tail. "I love hunting mice! But how come you're so hungry? You just ate a bacon strip! How come you need a mouse so soon?"

"Sapphie, you've forgotten everything we talked about last time."

The cat looked at Sapphie and licked his lips.

"Shadow, your teeth are pointier than mine. Can you teach me to make my teeth pointy, like yours? If I had pointy teeth like that, do you know how much more fun it would be to bite Zeph's ears?"

Shadow sat still. "Focus, Sapphie."

"Okay." Sapphie sat and wagged her tail.

"We're going hunting now."

"Okay. Wait. Why?"

"You've forgotten. Try to remember."

"You're hungry."

"Because...?" Shadow huffed.

"Because..."

"Think about what I told you last time."

"You need extra food because it's so cold out."

"And...?"

"And you're—" Sapphie tried to remember what they talked about last time, but mainly she just remembered all the interesting smells they found together. Besides, there were so many words to remember from last time, and Shadow didn't talk like a normal dog, so he was difficult to understand all the way. "Oh!" Sapphie jumped up. "You're having puppies soon! That's why you're getting so big! You need the extra food to feed all your puppies!"

"I'm a ca—" But Shadow sighed and shook his head. "Alright, Sapphie. Close enough. Let's go hunting."

Shadow walked—so daintily!—through the forest. Sapphie trotted along behind. "Shadow, you're the coolest friend I've ever had. When I grow up, I want to be just like you."

"Hush, Sapphie. Hunters need to be quiet and stealthy. If you want to be like me, you have to be quiet."

Sapphie tried her best to obey. She stepped exactly where Shadow stepped, trying to crinkle through the leaves as quietly as possible. Shadow froze suddenly, and Sapphie almost bumped into him. His ears darted back.

"Quiet, now. Steady. Steady."

Sapphie hunched low, trying to look like Shadow. She pushed her ears back, but they kept bouncing up. Her nose twitched, and she searched the area with her back legs extended, ready to pounce. She couldn't see what Shadow saw, but she could smell it. It was a warm little mouse hiding in the leaves. But there was something else Sapphie smelled, too. It was a pile of something dark brown and soggy, and it smelled intriguing. It would be great to roll in. Imagine if she smelled like that when Zeph came home. He would be so jealous!

"Okay, Sapphie, on my count," Shadow purred. "One." He bent lower. "Two." His tail flicked once. "Three." Without seeming to move a muscle, he jumped in the air and landed a few feet away on a pile of leaves.

As soon as he jumped, Sapphie sprang, too, but she didn't go for the pile of leaves. She went for the soggy pile of brown mush. She rolled and rolled and snorted and squealed. "This is fun, fun, *fun*!" she cried as she rolled on her back. She closed her eyes to enjoy just how pungent the smell was.

When she opened her eyes again, Shadow was standing over her, glaring. "You are very clumsy. Dogs are not good at being quiet. You made me miss the mouse. Your snorting and panting gave us away. You will return home now. Come back soon with another bacon strip."

Sapphie jumped up and wagged her tail. "Okay!"

"And Sapphie, you smell terrible."

"I know! Isn't it wonderful?"

Shadow started to walk away. "It won't be long," he said.

"Long?"

Shadow turned back. "Before the birth of—"

"The puppies!"

Shadow nodded.

Sapphie's eyes bulged out. "I can't wait! How many will there be? I can't wait to play with them. When I was born, there were four puppies. I was the fourth one, and cutest and bestest. Do you think there will be four puppies this time?"

Shadow huffed. "I wouldn't think too hard about it, Sapphie. Just bring me more food."

"Okay!" Sapphie heard her name being called, and she turned toward the cul-de-sac to see who it was. It sounded like Adam. "Hey, Shadow, do you think maybe my people would let you—"

But when Sapphie turned back, Shadow was already gone.

~ Thirteen ~

That night, Sapphie and Zeph sat next to each other, curled up in the bestest rocketship bed while the family watched that loud box on the other side of the room.

"Zeph, I have so much to tell you!" Sapphie yelped.

"I have so much to tell you, too!" Zeph nuzzled his sister. "I'll bet you got into the woods again."

"How do you know?"

"You smell like Maximillion's Pretty Puppy Shampoo. That means you got dirty and had a b-b-b—got cleaned, didn't you?"

Sapphie trembled a little. "Yes." Her eyes glowed. "But it was so worth it! I got to play with Shadow again. We even tried to go hunting. Didn't catch anything, though."

"Corgis, be quiet," Person Mom mumbled. "We're trying to watch something here!"

Zeph lowered his voice. "Sapphie, you know you can play with your shadow here, too. There's no need to run off into the woods."

"But Shadow can't come here."

"Why not? What's stopping your shadow from coming here?"

Sapphie cocked her head. "Maybe you're right. Do you think Person Mom and Person Dad would let him?"

Zeph sat up. "Why would they have a problem with your shadow coming here? It's not like you can help it. Your shadow follows you around all the time."

"You mean I follow him," Sapphie corrected.

"I guess you could look at it that way. Anyway, as long as you don't break anything, I'm sure you'd be allowed to play with your shadow inside. It's better than you running off into the woods."

"It *is* getting cold out there. I was wondering if it was too cold for Shadow."

"If it's too cold for you, it's too cold for your shadow."

Sapphie licked her paw, trying to remember the way Shadow did it. "This is a lot to think about. I'll have to think about if it's a good idea, and then I'll have to convince Shadow to come. I'm not sure if he will."

"Well, you'll have plenty of time to think about it and figure it out. You'll have many afternoons to yourself now. I got the part in Cassie's play. I'm working with Courtney for the next three weeks. I'll be playing the part of Denby Dog. I even got to try out my racer and everything."

"Hmph!" Zeph always acted like he was so smart.

"In fact, maybe I can show you how the cart works. It's kind of fun, actually. You might like it. I'm surprised you couldn't keep yourself together long enough to get the part in the play. Courtney and Cassie were talking about your behavior. Wetting the floor and chasing mice? I thought you were fully housebroken, Sapphie. And since when do you care about mice?"

"Shadow likes them," Sapphie said. "And if I want to pee somewhere, I can pee somewhere. I don't see what the big deal is. You're not the only smart one, Zeph. If I really wanted to, I could learn how to ride on that racer."

"Then why didn't you? Why are you bad all the time? What is Sir going to say when he finds out? And did you see how sad Courtney was yesterday? That was because of you, you know."

"Well..."

"Why can't you be good?"

"I am being good. I'm helping Shadow."

"A shadow doesn't need your help. Courtney does. Can't you see she's trying to be good? And you're making it ten times harder for her."

"But Shadow *does* need my help. He's always hungry."

Zeph growled. "Sometimes you make no sense, Sapphie."

"Sometimes Shadow makes no sense. I can't understand all the words he says. He doesn't speak like a dog, you know. He speaks like a c—"

"Hey, Zeph!" Adam called. He was walking up the stairs. Stupid Adam always had to get in the way. The same way he discovered Sapphie was loose this afternoon. And the nerve of him—to give her a b-b-b—to wash her delightful new smell away and replace it with Maximillion's Pretty Puppy Shampoo! And now here he was, interrupting yet again.

Zeph's ears perked up.

"Zeph, come on into the kitchen. Courtney said you did a real good job at rehearsal today."

"Really good," Person Mom added.

"And she's going to show me how good you move around in your cart."

"How well," Person Mom said. She liked to talk too much. "And I'd love to see him riding around in that cart."

"Hear that, Sapphie?" Zeph barked. "Come up in the kitchen with me, and I'll show you how my cart works. Maybe you can even try it."

"I know how it works," she snickered. But Zeph had already left. Zeph always thought he was so smart, but only Sapphie was smart enough to help Shadow. And she had to help him out in the woods, not in the house where there were bothersome busybodies like Adam and Zeph and stinky shampoo and crying Courtney. Things were much easier in the woods, and Sapphie couldn't wait to go back.

~ Fourteen ~

On Friday, the doorbell rang at 5:00 on the dot. Adam rushed down to answer it with Zeph following at his heels.

"Patrick!"

Patrick stood at the front door with a duffel bag slung around his shoulder and a Logan Zephyr and the Stellar Squadron sleeping bag at his feet. He looked even taller since the last time Adam saw him.

"Hey, Adam! Hey, Zeph!"

The corgi wagged his whole body. "Arooo!"

Coach Harris beeped the horn from his truck. "Nice to see you, Adam! Keeping that throwing arm in shape?"

"Yes, Coach!"

"Bye, Patrick. You boys have fun!"

"Bye, Dad!"

A cold wind prickled Adam's neck. Patrick shivered, too, and stepped inside. "I feel like it's been forever since we got to hang out."

"I know. It stinks that we're not in the same class. And you're always busy with baseball."

Patrick smiled. "I'm going to be stellar next season. Feel my arm!" He put down his bag, rolled up his sleeve, and flexed his arm for Adam.

"Wow. You're looking more like Logan Zephyr every day." Adam unrolled Patrick's sleeping bag and held up the life-sized image of Logan Zephyr, comparing him to Patrick. Patrick mimicked Logan's pose, and both boys laughed.

"You could be a superhero one day."

Patrick smiled. "My dad is having me lift weights."

Adam raised an eyebrow. "I thought push-ups were bad enough. I think my arms still hurt a little from your father's summer workouts for Autumn League!"

"Oh, he has me do plenty of push-ups, too."

Adam looked into Patrick's eyes. He seemed more serious than he used to be. "Are—are you still having fun? Training, I mean."

Patrick shrugged. "Sometimes. Other times, I get tired. But if I told my dad that, he'd get mad. All he has is me, and I don't want to disappoint him. I do enjoy baseball. It's just that sometimes I'd rather be doing stuff like reading comic books or relaxing."

"That's what tonight's for." Adam pointed to the family room. "We'll be sleeping in here. That way we can watch movies all night if we want to."

Patrick raised an eyebrow.

Adam sighed. "Okay, maybe not all night, but at least until my parents make us turn off the TV."

Patrick set down his bag, and Adam draped the sleeping bag over the end of the couch. "So tell me about this other kid. Gavin." Patrick seemed strangely serious.

Adam tried to lighten the mood. "Well, first of all, he has never read a Riley Couth comic book. Can you believe that? So we have to put that on our to-do list."

"Never?"

"Nope. He's really nice, though. He goes to Shepherd Meadow Elementary. He's a fourth grader."

Patrick raised an eyebrow. "A fourth grader?"

Adam nodded. "Oh, and I think he might want to play baseball next year."

"Is he any good?"

"I don't think he's ever played. But it seems like he might want to. He's a volunteer at the Stoney Brook Fire Company. That's where I met him."

"You like volunteering there? You sure you wouldn't rather join me for some off-season baseball training instead?"

Adam frowned. "Volunteering is only once per week, tops. Plus it's free. I know your dad's training you most days, but don't you also pay for classes?"

Patrick flexed his muscle again. "It's what the

winning teams do. Those boys from Altoona train all year, too. They pay plenty for private coaches. My dad's only paying for classes for me since he's my coach."

Adam frowned. "I think I'll stick with volunteering. But I can't wait until baseball starts up again. This cold weather stinks."

Patrick shrugged. "I kind of like winter. At least there's the chance for snow days."

"That's true."

"Arooo!" Zeph plopped himself at Patrick's feet.

Patrick sat on the couch and rubbed Zeph's belly. "I do miss coming over all the time like I did in the summer. I love playing with Zeph, too."

"You should get a dog. I can't imagine life without Zeph."

"I've been asking my dad, but he keeps saying we don't have time for a dog. It wouldn't be fair to leave the dog home all day while Dad's at work, and then leave him home some more while I do my training."

"That's true." Adam scratched Zeph's chin. "Maybe a cat?"

"I never thought about it, but a cat would be much more independent. You know, litter boxes and all. Or maybe I'll start small. Maybe he'll say yes to a hamster." Patrick looked around. "You know, I haven't been here since—Halloween."

Adam averted his eyes and sat next to Patrick. "Yeah, sorry about all that."

"Is your sister still in mega-trouble?"

"She's still kind of grounded for life. She has to volunteer at Willow Lakes on Saturdays. She's taking Sapphie to obedience classes on Friday evenings..."

"Is that where she is now?"

"Yep."

"I was wondering why it was so quiet—and why Zeph was so calm."

Adam laughed. "Yeah, it's much quieter without

Courtney or Sapphie. Oh! Courtney's doing this play after school. There's a character in the play, a canine, named Denby Dog. Sapphie was supposed to play the part, but she misbehaved real bad on the first try, so now Zeph's going to be doing the play instead."

"That's cool. I want to see it. Especially if your crazy sister messes up."

Adam nodded. "I'm going to the Sunday matinee. It's on December ninth, I think. Anyway, the play is being performed the day before, on Saturday, but I'll be volunteering at the firehouse that day."

"I'll ask my dad if I can go with you on Sunday."

"Cool. Maybe we can ask Gavin, too."

"I guess." Patrick stopped rubbing Zeph's belly, and Zeph snapped to a sitting position and howled. Patrick laughed and scratched Zeph's head. "So does Zeph have to go to rehearsal every day?"

"Cassie picks him up. He has rehearsal twice a week. I don't think he has to go every time. Courtney's supposed to write down the dates he has to go so Mom won't get confused."

"Sounds risky."

"You'd be surprised. Courtney seems to be turning over a new leaf. I'm giving her a chance."

"After what happened at Halloween, I'm not sure I'd—"

The doorbell rang, and Adam sprung forward. "That's Gavin. I'll get it!" Zeph jumped up, and Patrick followed. Adam opened the door to Gavin, who stood with a backpack and plain blue sleeping bag.

"Hi, Gavin! Come on in." Adam took Gavin's sleeping bag and closed the door against the cold.

"Arooo! Whooo!" Zeph jumped all over Gavin.

"Oh, he's so cute!" Gavin dropped his bag to pet Zeph. Zeph plopped onto the ground and rolled onto his back. Even flipped on his back, Zeph's little tail wagged.

Adam smiled. "He likes you, Gavin."

"I love him! I wish I could have a dog."

Patrick frowned. "That's what I said."

Adam pointed to Patrick. "Gavin, this is Patrick. Patrick, this is Gavin."

Gavin smiled. "Adam talks about you all the time. I can tell you're really good friends."

Patrick smiled at Adam. "Good to meet you, too."

The room grew quiet. Gavin picked up his bag. "Where should I put this?"

Adam pointed to the family room. "We're sleeping in there. After dinner, of course."

"What's for dinner?" Gavin asked.

"Pizza, I bet." Patrick smiled. "You guys always order pizza."

Adam grinned. "Actually, we're having tacos this time. Mom said we eat too much pizza. She's going to make them when she gets back, and we'll have a taco bar. She's trying to get us to eat more vegetables." Adam laughed. "But I'm only going to put cheese on mine. Anyway, Mom's with Courtney now at that dog training class."

Patrick laughed. "I'd give anything to see Sapphie behave."

Zeph barked.

"Oh, that reminds me, Gavin. Zeph has been invited to be in a play at my sister's middle school. Patrick and I are going to go see it. It's on a Sunday in December. You want to come with us?"

Gavin smiled. "Sure. I'm not sure if I can get a ride, though. My parents are probably going to be busy with the restaurant."

"That's okay. I'm sure they could drop you off here on their way to work, or maybe you could sleep over again."

"What restaurant?" Patrick asked.

Gavin's face turned red. "Apuzzo's. Business has been slow, and they've been working long hours until things pick up." His eyes lit up. "That reminds me, Adam. I thought about what Chief Kurle said. Remember he told me to use my brain to think of innovative ideas?"

"Yeah?"

"Well, I went home and thought about it, and I figured since it's November, maybe my parents could offer to serve Thanksgiving dinner at the restaurant. You know, start advertising and taking reservations. I'm sure there are lots of people who don't like to cook, or can't. Or maybe they have to work afterwards and don't have time to clean up. Anyway, they thought it was a great idea, so we're serving dinner on Thanksgiving!"

"I guess you're not going to visit your cousin, then?" Adam asked.

Patrick shifted from one leg to the next and looked up at the ceiling.

"No. We're staying here for Thanksgiving. My mom said we could probably do enough business to fix her car once and for all. I have to tell Chief Kurle next time I see him. I have to thank him for his encouragement."

"Thanksgiving dinner at a restaurant..." Adam rubbed his chin. "My parents said it will just be us this Thanksgiving since we're getting together with all our family over the Christmas holiday. I wonder if my parents would let us eat at your restaurant."

Patrick rubbed his stomach. "So when's your mom coming home? All this talk of food is making me hungry."

Adam checked the clock. "Soon. In the meantime, let's set up the sleeping bags, and maybe we can read some Riley Couth comics. You know, Gavin has never read one."

Adam ran upstairs to grab his sleeping bag, pillow, and fedora. When he returned, Patrick and Gavin were setting up their sleeping bags in silence. Zeph sat between them, cocking his head. When he saw Adam, he wagged his tail and scurried over. Adam cleared his throat. "Here's my Riley Couth sleeping bag." He spread it out between Gavin and Patrick's bags. "See how Riley and I have almost the same fedora?"

"Cool!" Gavin said. "I can't wait to read it."

Patrick made a muscle with his arm again. "And see how I'm getting to be just as strong as Logan Zephyr!"

Gavin smiled, but he looked down at his plain blue bag. "I've never read *any* comic books," he admitted.

"Mine are all upstairs. I'd bring them down, but I just heard my mom come home. We can't leave the comic books lying around; otherwise, the dogs might—" He stopped short.

"Might what?" Patrick asked.

Adam felt his ears burning. He remembered the incident involving a comic book Patrick had loaned him. It was an incident he wanted to forget, and one he had never truly told Patrick about.

Patrick raised an eyebrow, but luckily the conversation was interrupted by the entrance of Courtney, Sapphie, and Adam's mother.

"Hi, boys! Everyone hungry?"

But they could barely answer. Sapphie came rushing in, tackling Zeph and biting his ear. The two dogs barked and barked. It took Sapphie a minute to realize there were other visitors in the house. Then she took running leaps, saying hello to Patrick first, then to Gavin.

"How'd training go, Courtney?" Adam asked.

"Pretty good," she said. She averted her eyes. "Hi, Patrick," she mumbled.

"Hi, Courtney."

She kept her head low. "I'm going to go help Mom."

Adam leaned close to Patrick. "She feels bad about Halloween."

Patrick shrugged. "She shouldn't have done it, then."

"Done what?" Gavin asked.

"Why don't you tell him the story, Patrick? I want to go ask my mom something."

Patrick shrugged. "I don't like talking about it, but I guess it does make a good story."

"I'd love to hear it," Gavin said.

Adam hurried upstairs, with Zeph and Sapphie following. In the kitchen, his mother was already browning the taco meat, and the kitchen smelled delicious. "Hey, Mom, while you have a minute, I wanted to ask you about an idea I had for Thanksgiving..."

~ Fifteen ~

"If I eat another thing, I'm going to explode!" Adam said, patting his stomach.

"I don't even remember how many tacos I ate." Patrick sat on the floor with his back against the couch. Zeph sat at his feet.

"And an ice cream cone on top of it!" Adam sighed.

Gavin sat cross-legged on the floor, and Sapphie curled up in his lap. "Nice of Courtney to let Sapphie hang out with us." He smiled at Patrick. "That way we *both* get to play with a dog."

"Courtney probably didn't have a choice. Sapphie knew you were here, and she loves attention. She probably clawed at Courtney's door until Courtney let her out." Adam took a sip of his soda. "I'm so full, I don't even know if I can finish this soda."

"You have to," Patrick said. "Otherwise, you'll fall asleep. Sleeping's not allowed at a sleepover!"

The boys giggled.

Gavin's face turned red. "I have a secret."

Adam and Patrick turned to him. "What?"

"Um...this is the first sleepover I've ever been to."

Patrick raised an eyebrow. "Really?"

Gavin looked away. "I never had many friends. Everyone always seems to be into sports, but I never got into all that. It's like Chief Kurle said. I like thinking of ideas to use in business and stuff like that. I spend most of my Friday nights sketching or watching TV while my parents work at the restaurant. But I'm not even sure what's supposed to happen at a sleepover."

Adam smiled. "Nothing's *supposed* to happen."

"Yeah, you're just supposed to have fun." Patrick scratched Zeph's ears. "That's the point."

"I had fun reading about Riley Couth."

"If it were warmer, we'd be playing outside. Remember that time I slept over, Adam? It was summer, and we snuck outside at like three in the morning."

"We caught fireflies in a jar, and then we started a little campfire in my dad's hibachi grill and roasted hot dogs and marshmallows."

Patrick laughed. "Your dad got up for the bathroom, and he saw the flames. I never saw him run so fast."

"I thought we were going to get into trouble. I couldn't believe he sat out there and ate a hotdog with us. And the best part is, he never even told Mom!"

Gavin smiled. "That sounds like fun. I hope we can do something like that in the summer."

Patrick nodded. "If you and Adam are still friends."

Adam's smile faded. "Patrick!"

Patrick shrugged and took a sip of his soda. "Just saying. Everyone needs a best friend. You already have one. Gavin might find another best friend between now and next summer—you know, at his own school, or in his own grade—and then it'll just be me and you again."

Zeph flipped to his feet and looked at Adam. He cocked his head and whined. "It's okay, Zeph." Adam snapped his fingers, and Zeph sat in front of him. Adam scratched under his chin. "Of course you can come over in the summer, Gavin. I plan to volunteer for the fire company whenever I'm able. I do get pretty busy during baseball season, though. During the winter, I have plenty of time to do all my homework during the week. During spring and summer, it's very hectic."

Patrick smiled at Adam. "I can't wait 'til baseball starts again."

Gavin looked down at Sapphie. It looked like he wanted to speak, but he stayed quiet. Adam looked up at Patrick. "What else do we do at sleepovers?" he asked, trying to change the subject.

Patrick scratched his cheek. "We sometimes talk about girls."

Gavin swallowed a sip of soda, and his eyes bulged a little. "Girls?"

Patrick smirked. "For example, has Adam told you about Marnie Ellison?"

"Patrick!" Adam smiled, and his ears burned.

Gavin smirked, too. "Marnie Ellison?"

"There's nothing to tell."

"He went to a dance with her," Patrick said.

"Really? Does she like you? Did you kiss her?"

Adam felt his flushing ears spreading to his cheeks. His whole face was on fire. "I guess. She's nice sometimes, though she's mean other times—and very confusing. Yes, she likes me, I guess, and no—eww!—I didn't kiss her."

Patrick laughed. "The dance they went to was a Halloween celebration. They both dressed up in matching red sports costumes. It was very cute."

Gavin giggled.

"Alright," Adam said. "Time to change the subject again."

But Patrick was still laughing. "I've seen Adam and Marnie eating lunch at the same table this year. They're in the same class, and they seem to enjoy talking."

Adam searched his mind frantically for something else to talk about. He put his fedora on, pulling it low to hide his embarrassment. What would Riley Couth do? What would he use as a distraction? And how could he help Patrick and Gavin to become better friends? Adam's eyes flashed with an idea, and he chugged half of his soda. Then he smiled at Patrick and Gavin and burped, a loud, long burp that made Zeph skitter away.

"Excuse me," Adam said. "I guess I chugged that soda too fast." He smiled, hoping his distraction would work.

"That's nothing," Gavin said. He finished the rest of his soda. Then he burped, too.

"Ew, Gavin! That burp was disgusting! It smells like onions and salsa!" Patrick giggled, swallowed some air, and produced his own long, echoing belch.

Sapphie jumped at the echoing noise. Zeph growled.

"Ew!" Adam and Gavin cried in unison.

All three laughed. They swallowed more air and tried again. The room echoed with burps and giggles.

"Arooo!" howled Zeph.

Sapphie grabbed a stuffed mailman toy and ran around the room.

"We'd better be quiet," Adam said. "If we wake up my parents, they'll make us go to sleep."

The boys quieted, stifling giggles. Patrick let out one final burp, and the boys buried their faces in pillows to silence their laughter. Finally, they settled down and came out for air.

"Hey, it stinks in here now." Gavin held his nose. "Like taco burps and soda!"

"Like onions and corn tortillas!"

"Like soda and ice cream!"

Adam lowered his voice. "Go crack the sliding glass door open just a bit. Not enough to let the dogs out. We don't want them making noise this late at night. Plus, you never know when Sapphie will find a new way to escape. We'll leave it cracked open for a few minutes."

Gavin slid the door open. Sapphie and Zeph ran over, sticking their noses through the opening.

"Not until morning," Adam reminded them. "If you two are quiet, you can stay down here with us some more."

"I have an idea," Patrick said, sliding into his sleeping bag. "Let's watch movies all night. If we keep the volume low enough, your parents won't even come down."

Adam smiled. "Okay. Gavin, can you close the sliding door again? But don't slam it too hard, or it doesn't stay cl—"

Sapphie barked.

"Sapphie, hush!" Adam whispered. "You'll get us all in trouble."

Gavin shoved the door closed. Then he looked at the

clock and grinned. "I don't think I've ever stayed up this late before." He covered himself with his sleeping bag.

Adam picked up the remote controller. "We don't have to volunteer until later tomorrow. Patrick, don't you have practice in the morning? Aren't you going to be tired?"

Patrick yawned. "I'm always tired. I'll be fine. I'll ask my dad to go easy on me."

Adam shrugged. "Okay. Which movie should we watch first?"

~ * ~

Sapphie and Zeph snuggled into Zeph's rocketship bed. The boys were busy watching the glowing screen, and Sapphie needed to talk to her brother.

"Zeph, that was fun, fun, *fun*! Did you smell all those things coming out of their mouths? What are they?"

"They're called burps."

"Can you teach me to burp?"

Zeph sighed. "I'm not sure how to burp. I think only human boys can do it."

"Darn!" She snuggled closer to Zeph, but then she sat up. "Zeph, why is the door still open? Is the outside coming in to visit?" Her ear twitched with the idea. "And maybe if the outside comes in to visit, we can play, play *play*! And then maybe Shadow—"

"Sapphie, be quiet," Adam whispered from the other side of the room.

Sapphie whimpered.

"I think it had to do with a smell." Zeph's nose twitched. "I'm not sure I understand. I don't think Adam knows it's still open."

"You should bark to tell him."

"I can't. He just yelled at you for barking."

"So?"

Zeph's ears darted back. "Getting yelled at is the scariest thing in the world. I don't like it."

"Scarier than the outside coming in to play?"

Zeph shuddered. "Go to sleep."

"No way." Sapphie's nose twitched. "I think you're right about a smell. I think the door is open because the woods want to play."

"I don't think so."

"You sound like Shadow." Sapphie huffed. "No one listens to me."

"Shadow talks to you?" Zeph cocked his head. "What kind of stuff does he say?"

"Why don't you see for yourself? It's so cold out, anyway, and I'm getting worried. I keep wondering if we should invite Shadow to stay in here with us. It's much warmer, even though it isn't as fun."

Zeph sat up. "Sapphie, who is this Shadow? Or what? *I'm* getting a little worried. I thought you were just going into the woods to play with your shadow, but now I'm not so sure. Tell me about this Shadow."

"I *am* going into the woods to play with my Shadow. In fact, I'll go right now. Come on. I'll show you."

"Now?"

"Why not? When else will we both get to sneak out together?"

Zeph looked at the sliding glass door and trembled. "But it's so cold. It's so dark."

"Don't be a fraidy-dog. We'll be right down the street. Look, they left the door open a bit. We can push it open with our noses. And listen. Can you hear their breathing? They all fell asleep."

Zeph turned to look. "They fell asleep with that television on. I've never seen them do that before. I thought they were supposed to sleep upstairs."

Sapphie tugged his ear. "With that noisy box on, they won't even hear us sneak out. It's perfect! No one will catch us. We'll go out and sneak back in before anyone even knows we're gone."

Zeph paced to the door, but he stopped short and whimpered. "It's not a good idea."

"Come on, Zeph. Besides, if you stay here and bark about the door being open, Adam will yell at you. You said yourself that's the scariest thing in the world." Sapphie got up, rubbed against Zeph with her nose—the way Shadow would do it—and trotted to the door. She pushed her nose into the small crack and wiggled, opening the door wide enough to fit through. "Come or stay, I'm still going. Think about Denby Dog. What would he do? I'm just as brave as he is. Are you?" she asked before disappearing into the night.

~ * ~

Zeph sat trembling. He took a deep breath. He thought about the character he played, Denby Dog, and what Cassie said at all the rehearsals. Denby was so brave. Even with broken legs, he fearlessly tried new things. He inspired the other characters in the play to try for their dreams. What would Denby Dog tell Zeph to do? Would he tell Zeph to keep shaking and whimpering? Would he tell Zeph to curl up with Adam and go to sleep until morning? It was the fearless spirit, the spirit that drove Denby every day, that led Zeph and Sapphie to catch the sinister Mr. Frostburg over the summer. It was the spirit that blazed in Denby every day that allowed Zeph and his sister to help Adam during Halloween.

Zeph thought about acting more like Denby as he took another deep breath and followed Sapphie out the door.

~ * ~

Sapphie didn't even turn to look back. She knew that fraidy-dog Zeph would be only a step or two behind. She led him to the back of the yard, where the slat in the fence was still loose. Her people hadn't found it yet. She pushed through it with only mild difficulty. Zeph, who was a little bigger, had more trouble, but even he squeezed through eventually.

The night air was crisp. The ground had frozen just the tiniest bit, and in the moonlight the grass sparkled like Courtney's glittery toy. Sapphie licked it, enjoying the way the cool frost tasted on her tongue.

"Let's do this quickly," Zeph said. "I hope they don't wake up and lock us out of the house. It's cold out here. It could be morning before they know we're missing."

"Good! Besides, if you're cold now, imagine how Shadow must feel, being out here all the time."

Sapphie trotted across the front yard and down the street, heading toward the cul-de-sac. Zeph looked up at Cassie and Arabella's house. A light still burned in one of the windows. Someone was still awake in their house. Sapphie turned to her brother.

"Don't you think about barking at them for help."

Zeph whined. "How did you know I was thinking that?"

"Because it's what a fraidy-dog would do. Now come on, Zeph. Follow me. Shadow needs food. I didn't know we'd be seeing him tonight, or I would have saved him some. So if you see a mouse, catch it."

"Catch it? Sapphie, we're dogs. Dogs usually don't—"

But Sapphie couldn't wait. She hurried into the woods, ducking under bushes and underbrush and navigating through the trees like an expert.

"Shadow?" she whispered.

Overhead, an owl hooted. She heard Zeph shiver in the leaves.

"Come on, Fraidy. Shadow, where are you?" Sapphie froze. "Zeph, stay!"

Zeph froze, too, his ears perked.

Sapphie twitched her nose. She picked up a scent and changed direction. "This way!"

Zeph followed until they came to a small clearing surrounded by a circle of trees. There a dark gray bundle was huddled up in a pile of leaves.

"There he is!" Sapphie squealed.

Sapphie pointed with her nose, and Zeph inched over cautiously. There, snuggled in a bed of leaves, was the dark grey cat with beautiful glowing eyes that reflected the moonlight. The cat's ears darted back when he saw Zeph, and Zeph froze.

"It's not a shadow," Zeph growled. "It's a cat!"

The cat purred, then meowed. Zeph jumped backward.

"Of course he's a cat," Sapphie said. "Because he lives in the woods. We're cats now, too—because we're in the woods."

"Sapphie, that makes no sense," Zeph said.

"Sapphie, you still don't understand," Shadow sighed.

Zeph jumped back. "What a weird noise! What does 'meow' mean?"

Sapphie lunged for her brother's ear. "It's not just a noise. He's speaking."

"Speaking? That doesn't sound like any words I know," Zeph said. "I've never heard anyone say 'meow' before."

"I know. He sounds weird, and I can't understand everything he says all the time, but this time I understood." Sapphie growled. "This time Shadow agrees with you. You both think I don't know what I'm talking about." Sapphie licked her paw the way Shadow did sometimes. "In this case, you're both wrong. We're all in the woods, so we're all cats. When we go back into our home, we'll all be dogs. Because dogs live inside, and cats live outside. And if Shadow comes with us, he'll be a dog, too."

Shadow huffed. "Sapphie, that's not what we discussed."

Zeph jumped back and growled. "That weird noise again!"

The cat purred. "Tell your brother to stop being scared. Tell him I'm just a cat named Shadow."

"Quit being a scaredy-dog, Zeph. I told you. He isn't a shadow. His *name* is Shadow."

The cat meowed again, then purred.

Sapphie laughed. "And he said to tell you you're a silly dog."

"It's a cat." Zeph cocked his head as if he finally understood. "Every time you disappeared, you've been chasing a cat. Shadow is a cat."

Sapphie jumped up and down. "Of course he is! And look—" Sapphie stuck her nose into the leaves. "He's already had puppies!"

Zeph shook his head. "First of all, Sapphie, if a cat has had puppies, then he isn't a *he*, he's a *she*! And furthermore, if a cat has puppies, they aren't called puppies. They're called kittens."

"That's silly, Zeph. Those are too many words to remember."

"Your brother is smarter than you," Shadow said. "He's right."

"What!" Sapphie jumped back. "You're a *she*?"

"Of course I'm a she."

Sapphie cocked her head. "That's okay. I still want to be friends! I was wondering if you would come home with us and become a dog. You could bring your puppies."

Shadow darted her ears back and spoke to Zeph.

"Tell Shadow I still can't understand her," Zeph said.

"Shadow, Zeph says—"

But Shadow interrupted. "I can't leave my kittens now, but I could certainly use some help getting food. I would love a nice fat mouse. Did you bring me any bacon treats?"

"No, but if I get you a mouse, will you come back home with us?" Sapphie asked.

Zeph trembled. "I'm not sure you should be inviting her home, Sapphie."

"Don't be silly, Zeph."

Shadow licked her paw. "I might consider coming back with you, but not until my kittens are a little older."

"But it's so cold." Sapphie lunged for Zeph's ear.

"Zeph, make her come back with us."

Zeph barked at her. "I can't understand her, let alone convince her to come back with us. I think maybe you'd better go get her a mouse, if that's what the two of you were discussing."

"It *is* what we were discussing! Maybe you *can* understand him. I mean, her."

Zeph shook his head. "No, Sapphie. I'm just a good listener. Which is more than I can say about—oh, nevermind. Go get her a mouse."

"Will you help me?"

Zeph thought for a moment. "I've never caught a mouse before. I don't think I'd be very good at it. I don't think I'd want to, either."

"Oh, but it's so fun, Zeph. You have to be so sneaky—as sneaky as Sir!"

"No."

"Fine, scaredy. You stay with Shadow and her puppies, and I'll get the mouse."

Zeph cocked his head. "Okay, but hurry back."

Sapphie dashed through the woods, leaving her scaredy-dog brother and her new friend Shadow to sit in silence and darkness. She slowed her pace, letting her nose do the work. Finding mice was easy, and hunting was her new favorite thing to do in the world—more fun than even sleeping or eating!

~ * ~

Later that night, Sapphie and Zeph snuck into the back yard through the loose slat in the fence. They sat in the moonlight of the patio for a few minutes. As they spoke, their breath left ghostly trails in the air.

"Now I understand why you've been sneaking off, Sapphie. I'm proud of you."

"Why?" Sapphie lowered her front legs and raised her back, getting in prime pouncing position.

"I'm proud of you for saving some food for Shadow, and for going into the woods to help her."

132

"Wasn't that mouse I caught great? Isn't hunting exciting? Did you see the ways its tail—"

"Yuk, Sapphie. Let's not talk about that, okay?"

"Didn't you like it?"

"No."

"Shadow sure did."

Zeph huffed. "Good for her."

Sapphie lowered herself at Zeph's feet and rolled onto her back. "Are you gonna tattle-tale on me now? Are you gonna stop me from sneaking off into the woods?"

"No."

"No? Really?"

Zeph licked her ear. "I think you're doing the right thing. Shadow needs more food for her kittens. And it's so cold out. It's good she has you to look after her. I want you to try to convince her to come with you." He thought about Denby Dog. What would someone daring, someone fearless, do? Zeph snapped to attention. "We need to try to get People to come help her. It keeps getting colder out. It's up to us to rescue her."

"How will we do that?"

"I'm not sure, but I'll try to think of a way. For now, keep bringing her food."

"Zeph?"

"Yes?"

"If our People give you any more bacon strips, save them for her, okay? The only thing she likes more than bacon strips—is mice."

"That's asking a lot," Zeph said. "The only thing I like more than bacon strips is—more bacon strips."

Sapphie jumped up and pulled on Zeph's ear. "Come on, it's cold out here. Let's go in. The boys left that glowing box on, and I bet we could get away with sleeping on the couch for the whole rest of the night!"

~ * ~

Sapphie hurried inside. The sliding door was still ajar, and she slid in easily. Zeph took one last look at the mist forming like a ring around the moon. It was getting colder, and his breath came out of his nose in wispy white ghosts. He had to think of a plan for Shadow—and fast. Maybe the fire company could spare some extra fire for Sapphie's feline friend. His mind worked hard as he turned toward the house and followed his sister inside to the warm but forbidden comfort of sleeping on the couch.

~ Sixteen ~

On Saturday, Mom pulled up to the entrance of Willow Lakes without turning off the car. She and Dad had decided Courtney was responsible enough to be on her own at the nursing home for an hour. Courtney stood next to Mom's car and spoke through the open passenger-side window. She cradled Sapphie in her arms.

"I'll get some shopping done while you visit with Mister Grindle," Mom said.

"Okay. Are you going grocery shopping? You know, seeing if there are any good deals on food for Thanksgiving?"

Mom shook her head. "I forgot to tell you. You know Adam's friend Gavin?"

"I met him last night."

"His parents own a restaurant, and they're opening for Thanksgiving dinner. They're trying to get word out about their restaurant, and Adam tells me they're hoping to attract customers over Thanksgiving. I don't think many people have heard of the restaurant yet, so I thought we'd have Thanksgiving dinner there."

Courtney raised an eyebrow. "At a restaurant?"

"Why not?"

Courtney shrugged. "I always thought Thanksgiving dinner was at home. You know, home cooked meal? Sitting around and relaxing all day?"

Mom shrugged. "*Some* people get to sit around and relax. The other people get to spend all day in the kitchen."

Courtney nodded. "You're right. It sounds fun. I hope the restaurant is good."

"I hope so, too. So I don't need to do any grocery shopping for Thanksgiving, or for tonight. We're all going to Bingo night at the fire hall, and I thought we'd stop for chicken sandwiches on the way there. So I'll go to the bookstore while you're at Willow Lakes."

Courtney smiled. The mention of a bookstore reminded her of *Mister Baxter's Bookish Mess*. She couldn't wait for rehearsal on Tuesday. Things were going very well, and though she would never admit it to her brother, Zeph was doing a terrific job as Denby Dog.

"Okay, Mom. Just don't get lost."

"I won't. I have my GPS, anyway. I'll be back in an hour." Her eyes sparkled. "That reminds me. I know it isn't quite time yet, but I thought—since I'm leaving you on your own—I'd give you your phone early today. That way you'll have it in case of an emergency."

Courtney smiled. She took the phone. Sapphie sniffed it, licking its shiny case. "Eww, Sapphie." She stuck the phone in her pocket.

"I trust you'll be completely focused on your visit with Mister Grindle and the other residents, though. I trust you won't spend your volunteer time texting with friends. That would be rude."

"Okay, Mom. I understand. I won't even turn it on until I'm finished."

Mom nodded. "Good decision. You sure you'll be okay with Sapphie? You'll be able to handle her?"

Courtney hugged Sapphie. "She should be fine. She's exhausted this morning. I don't think she or Zeph got much sleep last night."

"I don't think Adam or his friends did, either." Mom smiled. "You know, the puppies slept downstairs with the boys last night."

Courtney raised an eyebrow. "Not in their crates?"

Mom shook her head. "And Adam—or one of his friends—left the back sliding door cracked last night. It's a wonder neither of the dogs got loose."

"Does that mean Adam's finally going to get in trouble?"

"I'll give him a talking to once his friends leave."

Courtney smiled. "Maybe you can wait until I'm

around to hear it."

"Oh, Courtney. I'll see you in an hour. Have fun."

Courtney waved as Mom pulled away. Then she put Sapphie on the ground and led her inside to sign in with Mrs. Bowers.

As usual, Mrs. Bowers was covered in pink. She bent down to pet Sapphie. "I'm so glad you're back. I love seeing your dog." Sapphie panted and plopped onto the floor, relaxing as Mrs. Bowers pet her. "She seems tired today."

Courtney finished signing in with the pink flamingo pen. "She stayed up all night, I think. My brother had a sleepover with his friends. He forgot to put Sapphie in her crate. We'll see if my brother gets in any trouble, though. I think this might be the first bad thing he's ever done in his life. He might start crying if he gets yelled at. I'm not sure he'll know how else to react."

Mrs. Bowers smiled. "Go easy on your brother. Everyone messes up. We're all human." She looked down at Sapphie. "Well, most of us are." She turned back to Courtney. "I just love your puppy."

Courtney smiled.

Mrs. Bowers smiled. "Now, if I might suggest, Mister Grindle had a great time with you last Saturday. He's got a bit of a head cold today, so he's in his room, but he asked if you might stop in and visit him." Mrs. Bowers winked at Courtney. "I think you made a new friend."

Courtney smiled. "Okay."

"He's in room two-hundred and two, down the first hallway, turn right into the two-hundred wing, and you'll see his room. Second on the left."

"Thanks." Courtney tugged the leash. She tried to keep calm and in charge. "Sapphie, come."

Sapphie followed immediately.

"Good girl."

Mr. Grindle was seated in his bed with his back propped up so he could look out the window. The morning sun streamed in and made his white hair look like it was glowing. He was cuddled under a blue blanket, and he had a book folded over his lap. His eyes looked serene and dreamy. Courtney wondered what he was thinking about.

She knocked on the open door.

Mr. Grindle awoke from his daydream and turned to her. His face stretched into a toothless grin. "Courtney! I was hoping to see you today."

"How are you feeling?"

"A bit under the weather is all. Just a cold. Miss Betty and my wife tag-teamed me to stay in bed today. Said I'll get better faster. Of course, Eleanor was too bored to stay in with me. She went down to the cafeteria for lunch. After lunch they're playing Bingo, I think. And then there's a quartet coming from the high school. I was looking forward to that. I might try to sneak out and watch it." He chuckled.

Courtney smiled. "Do music groups volunteer often?"

"Sometimes, but I wish I saw more of them."

Courtney scratched her chin. "Do other groups visit? Like, maybe acting groups?"

"We've never had an acting group." Mr. Grindle smiled. "But if someone came here to perform a play, I'd see it in an instant!"

Courtney reached for her phone. She wanted to text Cassie right away about this, but she stopped. Her phone was still off, and it could wait until she was finished volunteering. She smiled, thinking how Mom would be proud of her.

Mr. Grindle looked down. "There's little Sapphie!"

Sapphie barked at him, wagging her tail. She tried to jump up on the bed, but there was a railing on each side, and she couldn't jump high enough.

"She's so tired today. My brother had a sleepover and let her stay up all night. If she wasn't so tired, she'd be able to make it up onto your bed."

"I'd love to see her jump that high. Would you mind

lifting her? I'd love to have her up here with me. I do miss my dogs."

Courtney glanced into the hallway. "Are you sure you're allowed to have dogs on your bed? I'd hate to have Miss Betty come in here and yell at—"

Mr. Grindle dismissed her concern with the wave of his hand. "I'll tell you what. I don't know how much time I have left on this earth, but I can tell you that this morning will be made much better with a puppy by my side. If Miss Betty has a problem with that, then I have a thing or two to say to her." He took his arms out from under his blanket and crossed them across his chest. He smiled defiantly. "What do you say, Sapphie? Want to come up here?"

Sapphie barked.

"See?" He looked at Courtney.

"Okay." Courtney lifted Sapphie onto the bed. She jumped on Mr. Grindle. He scratched her behind her ears, and her whole body wagged.

Mr. Grindle smiled, and he wiped a tear from his eye. "I'll tell you, of all the things I miss, it's my dogs I miss the most. We all take things for granted, you know. When I was younger, I took it all for granted. How easy it was to run, to walk a dog. To move around without aching joints. To have teeth and be able to crunch into a cold raw carrot on a hot summer afternoon. That used to be my favorite snack, you know. Just the little things. That's what I miss the most. You young people should enjoy life while you can. Don't be like me. Don't take things for granted. Don't let other people keep you from being happy." He turned to Courtney. "Oh, listen to me babble on. You probably have no idea what I'm talking about, do you?"

Courtney tried to smile. She thought about her friends—Aileen, Noelle, and Meghan—and wondered if they were truly making her happy. Did she do things with them because those things made her happy, or did she do things with them because they wanted her to? She thought about *Mister Baxter's Bookish Mess*. That made her smile. That was something she *was* doing for her own happiness.

Mr. Grindle waved his hand. "Nevermind. So tell me, what's new in your life?"

Sapphie burrowed into the covers, and as Mr. Grindle scratched behind her ears, her eyes drifted shut.

"I've started rehearsal for a play I'm in. We had auditions this week, and even though things got all messed up, I got the part."

Mr. Grindle smiled. "Tell me about it." He pointed to a chair by the window. "Take a seat if you like."

Courtney smiled and sat down. By this time, Sapphie was sound asleep.

"The play is called *Mister Baxter's Bookish Mess*. It's about a man named Mister Baxter. He owns a bookstore—obviously. All these crazy, uptight customers come in looking for various things. One character comes in looking for candy, not realizing it's a bookstore. Another character comes in frantically looking for a how-to book about how to act on a first date. Then a pair of arguing siblings come in looking for a book that they hope will settle an argument they're having. A student comes in looking for a book to help him understand a book he was supposed to read for class. Then a teacher comes in looking for a book about how to get her students to read. It's a whole mess, and the point is, all the characters are super uptight, and everyone is worried about his own problems. They don't even see how silly their own problems are..."

"Sounds like my kind of play." Mr. Grindle smiled and continued to scratch Sapphie's ears. "What role do you play?"

Courtney smiled. "My name is Dani. Daring Dani. Obviously, I'm a daredevil. I'm a—what does Cassie call it? A foil character."

"What's that?"

"A character that's, like, the opposite of the other characters. A character that's supposed to show the other characters how they really are."

"In what way does your character do that?" Mr. Grindle asked.

"In the play, I have a broken leg. I got it while being brave, trying to do a trick jump on a skateboard. Obviously, it was a stupid thing to do, but my character is the only one who isn't upset and absorbed by her problem. So when the other characters see that and talk to me, they realize how silly they are being when they obsess over their own problems. In the end, everyone finds a solution to their problems, and everyone leaves the store a little happier than they came in."

Mr. Grindle smiled. "I wish I could see that play."

"Are you allowed to go out?" Courtney asked.

"It's hard for us to get around. Eleanor has her wheelchair, and with my cane I can walk at the speed of about a mile per day. We'll see, though. I'll ask Miss Betty. It would be easier if we had family nearby. Then we might be able to get them to take us."

Courtney smiled and reached for her phone to text Mom. Once again, she stopped herself. It could wait. Instead, she continued her story.

"The best part of the play is that there's a canine character—played by a real dog. His name is Denby Dog, and he's my dog, I mean Daring Dani's dog. He's got broken legs, too, and he's in a wheely cart the whole time, and he helps to calm everyone down with his positive attitude. Everyone sees how his injury doesn't really bother him or stop him from going for a walk with Dani, or chasing squirrels, or any other dog things, and once again all the people realize how small their problems are."

"Let me guess." Mr. Grindle pointed to Sapphie. "You got this little one to play the part of Denby Dog?"

Courtney shook her head. "I wish. No, I took Sapphie to the auditions, but she couldn't handle herself. She ran off backstage and tried to tear apart the school, basically. She peed on the floor and bit at the ventilation cover like she was trying to get in. The obedience classes have been working, though. I don't know what got into her. To make everyone's lives easier, we decided Zeph would get the part instead. Zeph's as boring as my brother. The two of them never do anything wrong."

Mr. Grindle held up a finger. "Didn't you just tell me that your brother made a mistake last night, letting Sapphie stay up all night?"

Courtney nodded.

"Remember, no one is perfect. Not even a dog named Zeph. Always remember that. If you start thinking the world is full of perfect people, you'll give yourself some kind of a complex like those characters in that play of yours. Understand what I'm saying?"

Courtney nodded. She turned to Sapphie. She was now lying belly-up and snoring quietly.

"She's out like a light." Mr. Grindle sniffed. "I should probably get some sleep myself. If you have time, you should stop by the cafeteria. I know Eleanor would love to see you for a few minutes, too."

Courtney reached for her phone to check the time, but instead, she used the clock on the wall. She had plenty of time for a visit to the cafeteria. "Come on, Sapphie."

Sapphie opened one eye, looked at Courtney, then fell back to sleep.

"I guess I'll be carrying her."

Mr. Grindle's eyes sparkled. "Hey, Sapphie. If you go with Courtney to the cafeteria, you might get some f-o-o-d. Food!"

At the word, Sapphie's eyes snapped open.

"Would you like some food?" Mr. Grindle asked.

Courtney laughed as Sapphie jumped up and barked. "Alright, Sapphie." She lifted the dog off the bed and took her leash. "Let's go to the cafeteria." She turned to Mr. Grindle. "I hope you feel better soon. I'll be back again next Saturday."

"I look forward to it." He turned back to the window. The sun kissed his face, once again illuminating his white hair. He closed his eyes again and fell into a smiling sleep.

~ * ~

Outside, Courtney sat on the bench and turned on her phone. Mom was already ten minutes late. She was probably in the bookstore looking for grammatical errors and probably lost track of time. Sapphie stretched out under the bench, awake but mellow.

When the phone powered on, Courtney saw that she had seven new text messages waiting. Before she opened them, though, she wrote a text to Cassie:

> **Courtney:** Want 2 talk 2 u about doing a play 4 nursing home.
> **Cassie:** Great idea! We'll talk @ rehearsal on Tues. :)
> **Courtney:** :)

Then Courtney texted Mom. She forgot how easy it was to send several texts each minute:

> **Courtney:** Where r u?
> **Mom:** You mean, "Where are you?" Grammar matters, even in texts.
> **Courtney:** *Sorry, Mom.*
> **Mom:** I'm still in the bookstore. I lost track of time. I'm on my way now.
> **Courtney:** Okay. Let's talk later about bringing Mr. Grindle and his wife to the play.

Mom responded with something uncharacteristic for her, and Courtney could hardly believe her eyes. Mom never used emoticons in her texts, or pictures, or anything like that, but this time, she responded with only one thing: a smiley face.

~ Seventeen ~

Bingo Night at the fire house was much less work than Spaghetti Night. Adam arrived early with his family. Mom and Dad had bought tickets for the event, and they brought Courtney, too. Adam showed the three of them to their table.

"I've got to go check in with Spencer," he told his family. "He's the head of volunteers. I'll come back out if I can."

"Okay, Adam." Mom turned to Dad. "While I'm thinking about it, did I tell you about Thanksgiving dinner?"

"That's next week already, isn't it?"

"Yes, and there's this restaurant owned by the family of Adam's friend, Gavin..."

Adam hurried back to the area in front of the kitchen. Spencer was there, as usual, with his clipboard.

"Hollinger, welcome back."

Adam nodded. "What's the plan for tonight?"

"Go check the bathroom for supplies, just like last time. When you're done with that, I think I'm going to have you help me with popcorn duty."

"Popcorn duty?"

"Bill was going to help me, but he just called. He can't make it tonight."

Adam frowned. He didn't want to say anything, but he knew Spencer hated when volunteers cancelled at the last minute. It was part of the whole speech he gave to the volunteers when Adam first started. Spencer must have read the look on Adam's face.

"Don't think I'm happy about it." Spencer tapped the clipboard. "This kind of last-minute cancellation throws the whole thing off. But it couldn't be helped. Bill had a bit of an emergency."

"Everything okay?"

Spencer nodded. "His family's washing machine broke. He and his dad tried to fix it, but they ended up causing a watery mess in the basement instead. They cleaned that up, but now Bill is stuck doing some painting for a neighbor to make a little extra money. They have to save for a new washing machine now." Spencer glared at Adam. "Don't you go around thinking it's okay to cancel your volunteering appointment once you've already committed, though. Bill has years in with this fire company, and this is the only time he's ever missed coming when he said he would."

"Okay." Adam shrugged. "So what's this popcorn duty?"

Spencer pointed to the buffet table. "As you probably know, if you've ever been to Bingo Night before, we serve popcorn to the guests. Each bag is sold for one dollar. As always, profits go to the fire company. Since I'm allowed to handle money now—I did a good job last time, according to Fire Chief Kurle—I was going to sell bags of popcorn and collect money, and Bill was going to follow me with the tray of popcorn."

"So that's what you want me to do? Carry around the popcorn?"

Spencer nodded. "Gavin's too small to carry it. Emily's in charge of making the popcorn. And Spark, well— she has her own duty for the night."

"What's she doing?"

"She did such a good job announcing tables over the microphone during the spaghetti dinner that Chief Kurle made her the announcer for tonight's Bingo games. He said he never met anyone so enthusiastic before. Apparently all the guests loved her. She's thinking about going into an acting career now—in addition to becoming Stoney Brook's first female firefighter, that is."

Adam smiled.

"I'll go check the bathrooms, then. And after that—"

"After that, you can relax until it gets a bit more

145

crowded. I'll come get you when it's time to sell popcorn."

Adam checked the bathroom quickly, then returned to his family. Mom and Dad were still talking about their plans. They had moved from Thanksgiving dinner at the restaurant to their travel plans over the Christmas holiday. Courtney sat staring at the table. Her cell phone sat on the table, and Adam could hardly believe she wasn't using it. He expected she'd be taking full advantage of the thirty hours of the week she was allowed to possess it.

"Bad reception?" Adam joked, putting an imaginary cell phone to his ear.

Courtney looked up. She looked sad. "No."

"Oh."

Courtney sighed.

Adam looked at his parents, but they were too lost in discussion to notice Courtney.

"Pretty soon we'll have some popcorn if you're hungry."

"Okay." Courtney rested her chin on her hands and sighed.

"Want to come see the fire engine?"

Courtney bit her lip. "Yeah," she said after a while. She stood up and put her phone in her pocket without even checking for new text messages. She followed Adam toward the back door.

"Everything okay?" he asked her.

"I guess."

"You're not mad that I left Sapphie loose all night, are you?"

She smiled. "Mom and Dad were mad about that, not me. You actually did me a favor. Because she didn't sleep very much, she was much better behaved at the nursing home and throughout the day."

Adam smiled. "Maybe it's because she was tired, but maybe it's because you're making good progress with her obedience training."

The corners of Courtney's lips drew into a small

146

smile. "Thanks, Adam." She sighed again. "It's just that, ever since Halloween, something just doesn't feel right when I text my friends. It's like we've broken a connection or something. It's hard to explain what it's like—not to feel like I fit in."

"I can understand that."

Courtney laughed. "That's right. I forgot my brother was also a nerdy little misfit." It sounded mean the way she said it, but Adam knew she wasn't trying to hurt his feelings. She looked so sad.

"I don't think you're a misfit. I think you're not sure where you *do* fit. You seem to like play rehearsals. Speaking of which, you're doing me some favors. With Zeph distracted, I can get my homework done much faster."

"Don't you have to watch Sapphie when you get home?"

"Yeah, but she mostly entertains herself. I let her play outside a lot. The worst part is that she rolls in so much stuff. I usually have to give her a bath when I finish my homework."

Courtney smiled. "I was wondering why she smelled so clean lately."

Adam opened the back door. "We can get to the fire engine from here." He led Courtney outside and jogged toward the huge garage.

Courtney pulled up the hood of her sweatshirt. "I should have brought my jacket."

"We're almost there." Adam opened the back door to the garage and led Courtney inside.

"This is Engine Ten, Stoney Brook's famous bright red fire truck."

"It looks so complicated up close." Courtney brought her hand up to one of the dials, but she stopped herself. "I didn't know there were so many gadgets and levers and dials."

"Neither did I, until I started volunteering here. I also didn't realize Stoney Brook's fire company, like most fire departments, was run by volunteers and donations."

"So that's why there are so many dinners and Bingo nights and all that?" Courtney asked.

"Yep."

"Wow. I didn't realize that. Makes me want to donate some of my babysitting money. Or maybe do some kind of a fundraiser for them. Like maybe put on a play." She reached for her cell phone. "Maybe I'll text Cassie."

While she turned on her screen, footsteps echoed behind them.

"Hollinger, what are you doing here?"

Both Adam and his sister turned around. There, at the front of the engine, was Spark. She wore her bright red SBFC jacket, as usual. She had painted several glowing red stars under her left eye.

"Hi, Spark. I was showing my sister the fire engine."

"It's called an *apparatus*," she huffed. "And it's not a toy."

Adam held up his hand. "I didn't think it was. We were just looking at how complicated it is and appreciating what all the firefighters have to learn."

Spark offered her hand. Courtney put away her cell phone and shook. "I'm Spark."

"Spark?" Courtney asked. "I'm Courtney."

"Spark is my nickname. My real name is Bianca, but I go by Spark. As in—cannot be extinguished."

Courtney smiled. "I like it."

Adam smiled. "Spark, I heard you're going to be calling Bingo numbers tonight. Congratulations."

Spark's smile stretched across her entire face. "Thank you. I did enjoy being behind the microphone last weekend. I think I might go into acting. I think my school's putting on a play in the spring."

"What school?" Courtney asked.

"Cold Spring Middle School."

"I go to Red Rose Middle. We're putting on a play in a few weeks."

"Hmmm. Maybe I'll come see it." She smiled. "You know, research my competition." She put her arm around Courtney's shoulders. "One day, the two of us could be competing for the leading role in some Hollywood blockbuster."

Adam laughed, glad Courtney was finally smiling. "I better get back before Spencer misses me."

"Why?" Spark asked. "What does he have you doing tonight?"

"I'm selling popcorn with him. He's collecting money. I'm handing out the popcorn."

Spark's eyes narrowed.

"What?" Adam asked.

"I don't know. Keep an eye on that guy. One day, *I'll* be in charge of volunteers, not him." She turned to Courtney. "Spencer's not sure who he is yet, you know what I mean? But me? I already know who I am, what I want, and how to get there. Ain't no one gonna bring me down. Now what about you, Courtney? Do you know who you are?"

Adam started to exit the garage, thinking that he should write something in his notebook about Spark's opinion of Spencer. But before he left, he turned around to catch one last glimpse of his sister. She was still smiling.

~ * ~

Adam made his way back to the window near the kitchen. The room was starting to fill up. Emily stood at the popcorn machine. It was already whirring and popping, shooting white and yellow kernels against the lit glass surface.

"Hi, Emily!"

Emily looked up from her work. She was counting red and white striped popcorn bags.

"Hey, Adam. I heard you're on popcorn tonight."

"Yep. I get to follow Spencer around." He smiled, but Emily didn't look up. "What are you doing?"

"Counting bags."

149

"Why?"

"Chief Kurle wants me to keep track of how many bags I start with this evening and mark down how many are sold."

"Why?"

Emily's face turned red. "Just for, um, accounting accuracy."

"Huh?" Adam paid close attention to her behavior, making a mental note to write it down in his notebook as soon as he got home—*red face, stuttering words, and failure to make eye contact*. Riley Couth would have a lot to say about that.

"Well..." Emily took a breath and finally managed to look up at Adam. "Let's say I have thirty-five bags here. If all thirty-five are sold, I'll end the night with thirty-five dollars."

"Right..."

"But if thirty-five are sold, and I only have *thirty* dollars..."

"Then that means five dollars..." Adam raised an eyebrow.

Emily nodded. "Walked off."

"Does Chief Kurle think that's been happening?"

Emily looked down again. "You didn't hear it from me, okay? And I wouldn't mention it to anyone. The more people you tell, the more likely the person responsible will be warned ahead of time—before he can be caught."

"He?"

Emily's face grew redder. "Or she, I guess."

Adam scratched his head. He wished he had his fedora and notebook. Here was a mystery! He had to list the suspects, record the clues...he should tell Gavin!

"What's Gavin been assigned to?" he asked.

Emily pointed to the table that normally sold raffle tickets. "He's been assigned to hand out Bingo cards to guests in exchange for their tickets. If they want to buy extra cards, they can pay at the table—one of the grown-ups is manning it—and Gavin will give them a card. He's also handing out Bingo stampers for people to mark their cards."

"But he's not allowed to collect the money himself?"

"Of course not. He's only in fourth grade, plus he's new here. No offense, but even as much as he likes you, Chief Kurle wouldn't even let you collect money."

"Likes me?"

"All he's been talking about around here is what a hero you are. He says you have the blood of a firefighter."

Adam thought about Patrick's strong muscles compared to his own. "I don't think I'd be a very good firefighter."

"It doesn't take just physical strength to be a hero, Adam. It takes something in here." Emily tapped her chest. "Kurle thinks you have that. But like I said, he's very picky about who he allows to handle money. In fact, he might be collecting money for Bingo cards and stampers himself. That way he can keep an eye on things."

Adam nodded. "I guess I should find Spencer." He hurried away, but he wanted to talk to Gavin first. He couldn't wait to tell Gavin about this mystery. The two of them could pretend they were in the middle of a Riley Couth adventure. But halfway to the Bingo table, Adam stopped short. Emily had told him not to tell anyone. And what if—it probably wasn't true, but what if Gavin was the one taking money? Patrick didn't seem too fond of Gavin, after all. And Gavin *did* mention that he wanted to be able to handle his own money. Adam's skin turned cold and sweaty. And didn't Gavin's parents need money for their restaurant? And didn't his mother need money to fix her car?

Adam shuffled back to the window near the kitchen, wondering what to do. He didn't have proof, but what if Gavin were the thief? How would he handle such a situation? He tried to think back to Riley Couth and all his adventures. Had Riley ever had to turn in one of his own friends? Adam couldn't remember a time, but there had to have been one. He made a mental note to call Patrick as soon as possible. Maybe Patrick would remember.

"Hollinger, where ya been?" asked a voice coming from the kitchen.

Adam turned around. Spencer was standing behind the kitchen window, holding the clear glass jar he had used to collect money last Saturday.

Adam looked down at his feet. "Sorry. I was showing my sister the fire engine."

"Engine Ten is not a toy, Hollinger. You shouldn't be there by yourself."

"We didn't touch anything. Besides, Spark was there, too."

"Oh, her." Spencer rolled his eyes. "Anyway, the place is getting crowded. Ready to sell some popcorn?"

Adam nodded.

"Alright. Grab a tray and follow me."

Adam hurried to Emily's table. She had filled several bags of popcorn and arranged them on a tray for Adam. The tray had a red strap that fit over his shoulders, making it easier to balance the awkward load. Adam smiled, remembering the way vendors sold popcorn at some of his baseball games. He sure did miss those days.

"Here." Emily helped Adam drape the strap over his shoulders. "Hold on," she said. She grabbed a glass of red liquid, which she spooned over several of the bags.

"What is that?" Adam asked.

"Cinnamon butter. I dyed it red for Lancaster. You know, the red rose and all. They'll sell first. You'll see."

Adam smiled and took the tray.

"Don't drop it, Hollinger." Spencer snarled. "Stay close."

Adam looked back at Emily. She winked at him. Then he followed Spencer into the crowd. He felt like he was at a baseball game, shouting, "Popcorn! Popcorn for sale! Get your popcorn here!"

~ Eighteen ~

Sapphie sat in her crate, staring at Zeph.

"Zeph, I'm bored. Where are our people?"

"They're with Adam."

"Where is Adam?"

"At the fire hall."

"What's a fire hall?"

Zeph growled. "We've been through this, Sapphie."

"Did it have to do with cats and puppies? Or maybe it was dogs and kittens?"

Zeph growled again. He tried to stay patient, but Sapphie made it difficult.

"No?" Sapphie barked. "Was it something about catching mice?"

"No, Sapphie. You're thinking of Shadow and the woods."

"That's right. Fire hall...fire hall...Oh! The fire company is the place that sells fire, which you need to heat up food. Right?"

Zeph barked. "Very good, Sapphie."

"So you think our people are buying more fire to cook us food?"

"Probably."

"How long does that take?"

"I'm not sure. I'm trying to think of a way to get some extra fire from the fire company."

"Why, why, *why*?"

"To give to Shadow."

Sapphie clawed at her crate. "That's a great idea. That will keep her and her puppies warm, right?"

Zeph nodded.

Sapphie spun around. "I don't want to be in my crate anymore. Want to break free and do something?"

Zeph trembled. "We're not supposed to."

"Come on, Fraidy. I promise we won't go anywhere. We don't even have to leave the kitchen. We can just run around."

"I don't think we should."

"Come on, Zeph. I'll give you my next bacon strip."

"No. You're saving those for Shadow."

"Oh yeah. I'll give you my ice cube next time we get one."

"No. It's getting cold for ice cubes."

Sapphie's eyes sparkled. "I'll let you rehearse your play for me."

Zeph's ear twitched. He was so excited to perform the play. How could he turn down the offer?

"Look, Zeph, your racer is there in the corner of the kitchen. You can even practice with it."

Zeph barked. Twice.

"I knew you'd see it my way. Okay, hold on. I'm coming." Sapphie raised herself onto her hind legs so that her mouth was level with the latch on her cage. With practiced skill, she slid the latch outward, then pushed it to her right. With a quiet *click*, the door popped open. She skittered across the kitchen floor to Zeph's cage, bit his latch, and let him out.

The two dogs scampered around the kitchen for a moment until Zeph remembered his cart. "Okay, are you going to watch me rehearse now?"

"Yes."

Zeph struggled to get his legs into their holsters. He fell over twice while trying. He twitched his ears. "It's easier if a person puts you in." He stood with his hind legs half-propped over the back of the cart. "You get the idea. It'll be a bit smoother the day of the performance when I'm all strapped in."

Sapphie growled. "Get on with it."

"Hush, Sapphie. I think you're jealous."

"Am not. I could have had your part if I wanted to."

"Why didn't you, then?"

"Because Shadow needed me. She still does."

"So you purposely didn't get the part?"

"Yes."

Zeph growled. "I don't believe you."

"It's the truth," Sapphie yelped.

"Fine. Sit quietly and watch, and tell me if there's something I can do better."

"Fine." Sapphie got down on all fours and waited for Zeph to begin.

"See, this is how I move around..." He scooted around in the cart, making three turns. "My first cue comes when Courtney says, 'Good afternoon, Mister Baxter. I'm looking for a book.' That's when I enter. I race down the ramp into the store, and then I bark twice at Mister Baxter.

"Then a bunch of customers come in. I'm supposed to howl at two of them. The first two. Then I ignore the second one, even when he talks to me. And then I'm supposed to chase the third one..." Zeph demonstrated his howling, ignoring, and chasing skills.

"Finally, at the end of the play, I leave with a bunch of customers, and Courtney stays on to recite some lines. When she says, 'I guess you never know how many lives you can change in any given day,' I race back on and bark three times. Then the audience is supposed to applaud. And that's the end of the play."

"Sounds boring," Sapphie huffed. "I could do all that."

"I wish you could see me perform it, but dogs aren't allowed at plays."

"It's okay. I should be with Shadow, anyway. It's getting even colder out. I hope you find a way to get more fire for her soon." Sapphie sprang up from the floor and tackled Zeph, cart and all. She bit his ears a few times. "Alright, fun's over, Zeph. Get back in your house so I can lock you in."

"How are you going to close your own door? You haven't learned how to do that yet. They're hard to latch from the inside, you told me."

"I'll pull my door shut. Our people are usually too distracted to notice much. You'll see."

Zeph whimpered and entered his crate. Sapphie pressed her front paws against the door and used her teeth to slide the latch through its hook.

"Safe and sound, brother." She barked with glee and took a celebration lap around the kitchen. "I'm still free, free, *free*!"

"Don't overdo it, Sapphie. Our people should be home soon."

But Sapphie didn't care. She barked and barked. She jumped on Zeph's racer and fit inside after several tries. Then she wheeled around the kitchen, yelping and barking the whole time. "This is fun, fun, *fun*!"

It wasn't until much later that she jumped out of the cart, panting heavily, and trotted back into her crate. She pulled the door closed as tightly as she could. "I've got to save my energy. Shadow needs more mice, and I'll have to do some hunting soon. Besides, if you find enough fire, it might be too heavy for you to carry by yourself, and you might need help!"

By the time the people returned, Sapphie was sound asleep.

~ Nineteen ~

On Thanksgiving morning, Adam sat in his room, fedora on his head. Zeph sat curled up on his bed. Adam was reviewing what he had written in his notebook when he heard a knock on his door, followed by a scratch.

"Come on in," he said.

Sapphie sprang into the room, followed by Courtney. Sapphie took a running leap onto Adam's bed and toppled Zeph, biting his ears. Zeph squealed.

Courtney held up her hand. "Sapphie, stop."

Sapphie stopped and barked once, then sat.

"Good."

"Wow, Courtney. She's getting much better." Adam put down his pencil. "What's up?" It was weird for Courtney to willingly set foot in Adam's room.

"Oh, not much. Mom told me to tell you we'll be leaving for Thanksgiving at noon. We have a 12:30 reservation. She thought we should eat early." Courtney's stomach growled. "Which is why she only let us eat an apple for breakfast."

Adam nodded. "Thanks."

"You're welcome."

Adam expected Courtney to leave, but she didn't. In fact, he wanted to be alone to consider all his clues. But Courtney just stood there. Adam raised an eyebrow.

"So what are you doing?" she asked.

"Going over some clues."

"Clues for what?"

He pointed to his notebook. "There's a slight mystery at the fire house, and I'm trying to solve it."

"What mystery?"

Adam squinted. "I'm not sure I can tell you."

"Why not?"

"I've noticed you and Spark have been chatting

lately."

Courtney nodded. "I think she's pretty cool. Even though we go to different schools, we have a lot in common."

"I'm glad you two get along, but that means there's a conflict of interest. You might reveal some of my research to her."

"What are you talking about?"

Adam picked up his pencil again and circled her name. "I don't think she's a suspect, but since she's involved in the fire house, I have to investigate her anyway. Riley Couth says never to—"

"What? A suspect for what?"

"Okay, okay, but you have to promise not to tell."

"I won't. It's Thanksgiving weekend. Spark and her family are busy. I won't see her again until—well, not next Saturday, either, since it's my play. I don't know when I'll see her next, and I'll be too busy with dress rehearsals next week to do much talking on the phone..."

"Okay. So Emily told me that Fire Chief Kurle has noticed a small leak in funds."

"Leak?"

"As in...money is walking away."

"Oh." Courtney bit her lip. "You mean someone's stealing."

"Yes. It's just a bit here and there. Last time, Emily counted the number of popcorn bags she made and the ones that were sold. There was a discrepancy of ten bags, meaning ten dollars simply vanished. And Chief Kurle doesn't let just anyone handle the money. Even Emily isn't allowed to. The only person he trusts who isn't an adult is Spencer. And Spencer's worked hard to earn that trust. So the criminal could be an adult. Then again, it could be a younger volunteer who sneaks a few dollars when no one's looking. Could be Spencer, too."

"Maybe someone made a mistake giving change?"

Adam shook his head and pointed to his notebook.

"When I first volunteered at the fire company, it was mentioned that things sometimes went missing. I think someone's doing it on purpose."

Courtney sat on the bed next to Sapphie and Zeph, scratching one puppy with each hand. Both puppies plopped down and immediately started closing their eyes. "So who's your prime suspect?"

"I haven't been able to rule out anyone yet. I wouldn't think Emily would have done it. I have reason to suspect Gavin, though."

"What? Your friend? Are you crazy?"

Adam frowned. "He needs money for his family. He's always complained that his mom never lets him handle money himself. And when I talked to Patrick about him, Patrick seemed to think Gavin was a prime suspect."

Courtney laughed. "You really aren't that bright when it comes to friends, are you, Adam?"

"What do you mean?"

"Can't you see what's going on? I could see it during the two seconds I talked to Gavin and Patrick during your sleepover."

"What are you talking about?"

Courtney huffed, and the dogs awoke. She lowered her voice, and they soon fell back to sleep. "Patrick's your best friend, right?"

"Of course."

"And who have you been spending more time with lately, Patrick or Gavin?"

"Well...Gavin. But that's only because—"

Courtney held out her hand. "It doesn't matter why. The fact is, Patrick sees that his best friend—you—is spending more time with someone else. Don't you think he's a little jealous?"

Adam looked back at his list. "I never thought of it that way."

"Didn't you think Patrick was acting a little strange at the sleepover?"

"A little, I guess, but I thought he was just tired from all the training his dad's been making him do."

Courtney shook her head. "That's jealousy. Believe me, Adam. I've spent so much time with friends who were all about gossip, jealousy, and plotting—I know jealousy when I see it. You should talk to Patrick and let him know the two of you are still good friends. Maybe plan an activity with just you and him sometime."

"Hmm."

"Now who else is on your suspect list, Adam? I'm a little worried. You don't think Spark—"

"I don't think Spark would steal anything from the fire company. If nothing else, it would ruin her chance of being a firefighter one day. But still, she works there, so I can't rule her out completely."

"Are you a suspect?"

"Of course not," Adam said.

Courtney laughed. "How can you be sure?"

"Courtney! I would know if I stole money from the fire company!"

Courtney shrugged. "What about this Emily person?"

Adam shook his head. "Emily wouldn't steal anything. Fire Chief Kurle trusted her to help him figure out who was stealing."

"You sure about that?"

"Yes."

"Really? Do you have proof that she's innocent?"

Adam thought about Riley Couth. Riley often trusted his gut, but he also always found evidence to support his feelings. "Well, I—"

"Don't rule anyone out is all I'm saying. Isn't your big crab leg feed coming up? I'm sure you'll be able to find more clues then." Courtney got up and gave Adam's head a friendly tap, knocking his fedora onto the desk. "Don't think too hard about it. Remember to have fun, too. Come on, Sapphie. Adam, Mom is freaking out about being on time. She wants us to let the dogs out at 11:45. I'll let them out if you let them back in just before we leave. Deal?"

"Deal."

~ Twenty ~

The restaurant owned by Gavin's parents, Apuzzo's, was booked solid. Gavin smiled as he greeted the Hollingers at the front entryway.

"Welcome to Apuzzo's!" he said. He wore a formal suit with a red tie. "And Happy Thanksgiving!"

Mom smiled at him. "Happy Thanksgiving to you, too. Your parents have you working?"

Gavin smiled. "They said I would get a percentage of the tip money if I helped out. My job is to greet guests, show them to their tables, and help clear the tables after everyone's done." He turned to Adam. "I think I'm going to spend my money on comic books."

Adam smiled.

Gavin grabbed four menus and led the Hollingers to a table near the window. The restaurant was decorated in rich red and brown velvet. It felt upscale but comfortable. Gavin held the chair for Mom and Courtney. Courtney blushed.

"Now for Thanksgiving, we have two menus to choose from. The right side of the menu features a traditional holiday meal—turkey, mashed potatoes, and all the fixings. The left side of the menu features the best of our restaurant—Italian cuisine at its finest."

"Is your family Italian?" asked Dad.

"Yep. We're the Apuzzos. The recipes we use were passed down from my grandmother, and she learned them from her family in Italy."

"Well, I can't see eating anything other than turkey on Thanksgiving," Dad said.

Gavin frowned.

"But I'm sure the Italian food is good, too."

Gavin nodded. "It is. In fact, it was my idea to offer an Italian menu today. My parents were going to focus on turkey, but I told them if they offered an Italian menu, we could show off the food we normally serve."

"Mozzarella cheese sticks!" Courtney said. "Those are my favorite. I'm definitely ordering from the Italian side."

"I am, too," Mom said. "I'd love a taste of Italy." She looked at Dad. "And I'm sure you'd let me try your turkey?"

"Of course, dear." Dad smiled.

"Adam, what about you?" Gavin asked.

"I'm not sure yet."

He smiled. "In any case, all the meals come with a salad, so I'll send your server out to take drink orders and bring out salads."

Gavin bowed and hurried away to greet the next set of guests.

"What an industrious young man," Dad said. "He's got a mind for business, I'll tell you that. He acts more professional than people twice his age."

Adam reminded himself to write Dad's observation in his notebook. He wondered if someone who was described as "industrious" would try to steal money from a fire company.

He looked at Courtney, but she seemed to be reading his mind. She shook her head.

Mom looked at her watch. "For once, we're exactly on time. We were here at twelve-thirty on the dot."

"No thanks to Adam," Courtney said. "You were so busy writing in that notebook of yours, you almost forgot to let the dogs back in."

"But I did—even if it was at the last minute." Adam smirked. "I let them in, closed the door, and got them into their crates in record time!"

"Practicing hustling for baseball already, huh?" Dad smiled.

"Can't wait," Adam said as the waiter arrived to take their order.

After they ordered—Adam decided on turkey after all—Mom smiled at Dad and then turned to Courtney.

"Courtney, we wanted to save this announcement for Thanksgiving dinner because we wanted it to be something special." She smiled at everyone. "We have a lot to be thankful for lately."

Dad continued. "Courtney, we've noticed you've been more responsible lately. Sapphie's behavior has been improving. We can tell you've been working with her on her training."

"And we've noticed you're spending more time on your schoolwork."

Courtney nodded. She looked nervous.

Mom put a hand on Courtney's arm. "Mrs. Bowers also tells me you've been so kind at the nursing home. Supposedly you've made Mister Grindle's day several Saturdays in a row." She turned to Dad again.

He cleared his throat. "We were thinking that we would give you full phone privileges back at the start of winter break."

Courtney smiled, but Adam could tell it was forced.

"Isn't that great?" Mom asked.

"Yes," Courtney said.

Dad turned to Courtney. "Now, we expect you to keep it off while you're at school. And we expect you to keep up the same level of focus on your schoolwork." He nodded. "And you'll still be responsible for volunteering every Saturday at the nursing home. Sapphie's classes end right before Christmas, so as long as her behavior remains good, you'll just have to keep up her training on your own. But until and unless she needs more schooling, you won't have to take her to obedience classes anymore after that."

Mom bit her lip. "Although, I was talking to the trainers. They seem to think Sapphie is very smart, and that her behavior is the result of boredom."

Courtney laughed.

"I'm serious. They think you should consider agility

training for Sapphie."

"What's that?"

Adam smiled. "I read all about it. It's doing stuff like running after balls and jumping over things. There are all kinds of contests you can enter. You can even earn money if your dog is good enough. There are some team events and some individual ones."

Courtney frowned. "You really think Sapphie can handle that?"

Mom and Dad laughed. "She's found numerous ways to escape from our yard. I'm sure she'll be able to figure out how to jump."

Courtney nodded. "I'll think about it." She took a sip of water. "I wanted to talk to you about something else." Her face grew serious. "I'm really enjoying acting in this play. I think I'd like to continue acting, if possible. Red Rose Middle School usually has a spring play, and I plan on auditioning."

"I think that's great, Courtney. And if you continue with chorus, the high school always performs wonderful musicals. Maybe you could be involved in those." Mom's smile widened. "I'm so proud of you, Courtney. You're really finding your way."

"The other thing..." Courtney took a deep breath. "It has to do with Mister Grindle."

"Who?" asked Dad.

"Mister Grindle, dear," said Mom. "He's the man at the adult living facility I was telling you about."

"Oh, *that* Mister Grindle. The one at Willow Lakes!"

"Yes." Courtney continued. "He really wants to see a performance of *Mister Baxter's Bookish Mess*, but his family lives too far away to take him. See, it's hard for him and his wife to get around. But I was wondering if maybe we could...invite him along. You know, to see me during the matinee? I've already been talking to Cassie about coming up with a play to perform at Willow Lakes, but for now— because there are so many actors in the play, I think it would be easier to bring Mister Grindle to the play."

Mom's eyes watered, and she dabbed at them with a napkin. "Oh, Courtney! I'm so proud of you. Of course he can come. I'll contact Willow Lakes tomorrow to see about making arrangements. I'm sure it will all work out. Oh, this will be great!"

Adam cleared his throat. "I was going to invite Patrick and Gavin to the play that day, too."

"It'll be a full house," Dad said. "We may have to take two cars."

"It'll be lots of fun." Mom turned to Adam. "And tell us about the plans *you* have for next weekend. What is it Fire Chief Kurle has planned with Zeph?"

Adam smiled.

"Fire Chief Kurle read all about me last summer. He says I have the blood of a hero."

Mom and Dad smiled. Mom wiped her eyes again.

"He wants to have a photo session with Zeph. People will make donations to the fire hall in exchange for a picture with the famous dog."

Dad smiled. "We're proud of you, too, Adam. You've been very responsible lately."

Courtney smirked. "Except for leaving the dogs loose all night and leaving our sliding glass door open. Mom and Dad are always nagging me about the heating bill, telling me to put on an extra sweatshirt, and here you let the cold air come in all night."

"Courtney." Mom clicked her teeth. "Everyone makes mistakes. Adam, I'm sure you know now to make sure that sliding glass door is always closed. You know if you slam it too hard, it bounces back open."

Adam nodded. Mom turned to Dad. "Should we tell him now?"

Dad nodded.

Mom turned back to Adam. "Adam, when Courtney gets her phone back at the beginning of Christmas break, we're also going to give you your very own phone. With you being so busy all the time, we thought it would be important for you to have a way to contact us. It will have a simple texting and calling plan. Nothing fancy, but we figured it would be a nice first step. For our volunteer, scholar, and baseball star."

Adam smiled. Several of his friends had their own phones, and he couldn't help imagining what it would be like to have one of his own.

"We wanted to tell you now so you can help pick out the style you like. Maybe we'll go shopping sometime the week after next—after everyone's busy schedules calm down a bit."

"Thanks." Adam felt his ears getting red. "That'll be cool."

"Courtney, since you're the phone expert, we thought you could help your brother pick one out."

Courtney smiled.

Mom insisted on saying grace when the food arrived. She started tearing up again, expressing thanks about how wonderful her two children were turning out to be and how she knew they would go on to do great things in the world. Luckily, Gavin was nowhere in sight to see how red Adam's face became. In fact, Adam didn't see Gavin any more that afternoon, except running back and forth to greet guests. But the food was delicious, and Adam and Courtney were getting along for once. The Hollingers had much to be thankful for, and all was right with the world.

Until they got home.

~ Twenty-One ~

Adam could tell something was wrong as soon as they opened the front door. Zeph was in the kitchen, barking like crazy, and the house was cold and smelled like late autumn.

"What's going on?" Mom asked.

Courtney ran up to the kitchen. A moment later, a shriek echoed through the house. "Sapphie is missing!"

Dad held up his hand. "Everybody calm down. I'm sure there is a rational explanation for this."

"The burglar must be back!" Courtney sniffed away tears. "And this time he stole Sapphie!"

"No way." Adam ran up to the kitchen to check on Zeph. He was still securely locked in his crate. He stopped barking when he saw Adam. "If someone did break in, why would he steal Sapphie and not Zeph?"

"Because she's cuter!" Courtney shouted before breaking down in tears.

Dad came up from the family room. He held his hand on his forehead. "The back sliding door was open."

"See?" Courtney sobbed. "Someone broke in."

"Courtney, calm down. They couldn't have gotten in that way. Someone here must have left the slider open accidentally."

All eyes turned to Adam. His ears caught fire immediately. "I—I—"

Mom put her hands on her hips. "Adam Hollinger, you know that if you slam the sliding door with too much force, it bounces open again."

"I know, Mom. I didn't mean to. I was in such a rush to get to the car. I didn't want to make us late. I guess I didn't stop to make sure it was closed and locked."

Dad rubbed the back of his neck. "I should have fixed it. I've been meaning to. I mean, especially after the burglaries this summer, I should have made it a priority. I've been so busy with work lately. I need to limit myself to a set schedule so I have more time to—"

"Not now, Doug." Mom pointed to Courtney. "Right now, we have to find Sapphie." She turned to Adam. "Put Zeph on a leash. I'll bet Zeph will lead us to her."

Adam hurried, and before long, Zeph was on the end of a leash, pulling Adam out the front door. He was followed closely by Courtney, Mom, and Dad.

"Sapphie!" Courtney called.

"Sapphie!" called Mom and Dad.

"Zeph, find Sapphie!" Adam said.

Zeph hurried to the cul-de-sac and continued toward the woods. Adam turned to his parents. "He wants to go in there."

"Should we let him?" asked Mom.

"Of course you should!" Courtney jumped up and down. "Sapphie's in there. He can find her!"

"I can't leave him on the leash." Adam pointed to the underbrush. "He'll get all tangled up."

Dad crossed his arms. "Let him loose, Adam. He knows what to do. He won't run off."

Adam looked at Mom.

"Alright," she said. "But after this, we all have to check ourselves for ticks. And the dogs, too."

Adam took a deep breath. "Okay." He knelt down. "Zeph, go find Sapphie, but don't run off or get lost. I don't know what I'd do without you."

He unclipped Zeph's leash and exhaled as Zeph leapt through the underbrush.

"Follow him!" Adam shouted.

They dashed through bushes and leaf piles. Adam heard critters scampering through the dried leaves, but he didn't stop to think about the snakes and other creatures that could be hiding. He kept Zeph in sight. His pants tore on a briar bush, and he felt the pricker dig into his skin, but still he didn't stop.

"I have the blood of a hero in me," Adam whispered as he ran. He looked behind him. Mom and Dad were standing at the edge of the woods. Even Courtney stopped, not sure how to make her way through the undergrowth. "Don't worry," Adam called to his family. "I'll catch up with Zeph and find Sapphie. You just be ready with Sapphie's leash!"

"Okay, Adam!" Courtney called. "Please find her. It's so cold out. What if she's frozen?"

Adam leapt over briars and bushes, keeping right on Zeph's tail. He ducked under trees and around pines. Just as he slid on a pinecone, Zeph came to a screeching halt.

"Did you find her?"

Adam knelt down. There was Sapphie, cuddled up next to a gray cat. Adam steadied his breathing. "Sapphie?"

Sapphie looked up, but she didn't make any sound. The cat looked up briefly but lowered its head again.

"Is she hurt?" Adam reached to the cat. It bared its teeth at him for a moment, but then it lowered its head again. Sapphie stood up briefly, long enough for Adam to see several tiny, sleeping kittens nestled underneath their mother.

Adam's eyes popped open. "Kittens!" He turned to Zeph. "Zeph, Sapphie, stay. I'll be right back."

Zeph barked once, but he sat next to Sapphie and watched Adam leave.

"Mom! Dad! Quick! Get a box! Sapphie found a cat, and it had kittens!"

"In this cold weather?" Mom shouted.

Adam watched her run toward the house, but Cassie and Arabella shouted from their porch on the hill. "What's going on?"

"A box!" Mom called to them. "We need a box and a comforter!"

Courtney was jumping up and down. "Where's Sapphie?"

"Sapphie and Zeph are guarding the cat. I think

they'll let us take the kittens. The cat seems pretty weak. Hopefully she'll let us help her."

Mom came back with the box. Adam reached for it, but Dad took it instead.

"Let me do this. The cat could be sick, or rabid, and if it is, I don't want you getting hurt."

"Rabid!" Courtney broke into renewed tears. "But Sapphie's been with that cat!"

Mom put an arm around Courtney. "It's okay. She's had all her shots. And I'm sure the cat's fine. Adam, didn't the cat look fine?"

"Fine—but tired," Adam called as he followed Dad through the woods.

He was out of breath when he reached Dad, who knelt over the cat. Zeph ran up to Adam.

"Arooo!"

"Good boy, Zeph."

"Adam, take Sapphie, please."

"Sapphie, come here, girl."

Sapphie looked at Zeph. Zeph barked. Slowly, Sapphie stood and shuffled toward Adam. Then she sat and watched.

Dad held out his hand toward the cat.

"What are you doing?" Adam asked.

"Letting the cat sniff me."

"I think that's how dogs work."

Dad shrugged. "I've never had a cat before. I'm not sure *how* they work."

"Well...be gentle with her, okay?"

"I'm going to take your kittens and get you help." Dad showed her the box.

"I don't think she understands that."

Dad reached for the first kitten. The cat hissed and bared her teeth. Dad snatched back his hand. Zeph barked.

"You're right. She doesn't understand."

"Maybe we should call for help."

Dad shook his head. "It's Thanksgiving. Most places

are going to be closed."

"Maybe we can wait until tomorrow. The cat's survived this long."

"It's been getting colder every night, Adam. We should try to get her inside. And we'll have to get the kittens to the vet."

Adam turned to Zeph. "Zeph, what do we do?"

"Arooo!" Zeph cried.

"You don't have any ideas either, do you, Zeph?"

"Arooo!"

Sapphie barked.

"Sapphie, what about you?"

Sapphie pranced over to the cat. "Rooo!" Sapphie howled.

Dad and Adam exchanged glances.

"What was that?"

Adam shrugged. "I've never heard her make that sound before."

"Rooo!" Sapphie howled again.

Slowly, the cat shifted her weight. Dad slowly brought his hand closer to the kittens. This time, the cat stayed still, but she watched Dad's every move as he gently lifted each tiny kitten into the box.

"What about the cat?" Adam asked.

Dad handed Adam the box of kittens. "Carry them carefully. The corgis will follow you. I'm going to try to pick up the cat." He held out his hands. "Here, kitty, kitty."

"Dad, I don't think that really works."

Dad reached toward the cat and picked her up gently. She remained relaxed in his arms and even cuddled against his chest.

"Alright," Dad announced. "I think we're ready to go home. Sapphie, Zeph, let's go."

~ * ~

That evening, Courtney sat at the kitchen table staring at the large cardboard box in the corner of the kitchen. Dad had lined it with Cassie's comforter, and the cat snuggled with her kittens. Mom had set out a saucer of milk and some cut-up strips of chicken. The cat had eaten a bit but seemed more content to rest somewhere warm.

"I finally got a call back from the vet's answering service. They open again tomorrow morning, and they said we should bring the cats in right away to see if they're healthy."

Dad cleared his throat. "Who's going to pay for all that?"

"Oh, Doug!" Mom huffed out of the kitchen, followed by Dad.

Courtney sighed, not wanting to be involved in an argument between her parents. She turned to Sapphie, who hadn't left the side of the cardboard box—or the cats—since they'd been put in the kitchen.

"Sapphie, Mom thinks you're super smart and just being bad because you're bored. Is that true?"

Sapphie looked up only briefly, sighed, and then turned back to the cats.

"I find it hard to believe, too. But sometimes I wonder. I mean, after something like your little escape today...it almost seems like you did it on purpose."

Sapphie shifted her eyes, but she stayed next to the box.

"I wonder if you could have been good enough to be in the play. You know, I don't mind working with Zeph, but you're my puppy, Sapphie, and I would have rather been spending time with you. I'm not sure if you can understand me, but—" She sniffed. "I'm not even sure who my friends are anymore. Aileen, Noelle, and Meghan don't seem to be the good friends I remember them to be. It's like everything I thought I could count on—I can't count on any more. But I always thought I could count on you. Even if you were being bad, at least I knew I could count on that. At least I knew you were being honest. But now, if Mom's right, if you're doing bad things on purpose, then I'm not even sure I can count on my own dog."

Courtney sniffed a few more times. "You can sit here and guard your cats, then. I'm going to bed. When Adam brings Zeph to bed, he'll put you in your crate, too."

She sniffed upstairs without petting Sapphie goodnight. She hoped her dog would follow, but Sapphie only whimpered and sighed and stayed near the cats.

~ Twenty-Two ~

On December seventh, the evening of the crab feed, Adam stood in front of the mirror. He wore his Stoney Brook Fire Company t-shirt and his matching red Lancaster Reds baseball cap. He practiced smiling and turning his head one way or another, trying to choose the best angle for his pictures with Zeph. Finally, he went downstairs to look for Mom.

She was nowhere to be found.

"Courtney, where's Mom?" Adam asked when he passed Courtney's room.

She pulled out her earbuds. "What?"

"Where's Mom?"

"I don't know. I think she's at the vet."

"Again?"

Courtney shrugged.

Adam scratched his head. "But isn't Mom supposed to be bringing me to the crab feed?"

"I don't know. There was some emergency at the vet today. She couldn't take the cats in until after I got back from Willow Lakes. They must be busy today. The cats needed shots or something, and she was going to ask about getting them adopted—unless Cassie and Arabella get attached and want to adopt them all. Cassie's coming over in a minute or two to give me a ride to the school. Our show starts at seven o'clock. Mom's meeting us there."

"I hope she has time to drop me and Zeph off first..."

But Courtney already had her earbuds back in. Her lips moved as if she were reciting her lines, so Adam left her alone.

He checked the time. It was 4:15. If he was going to be on time, he had to leave soon. "Come on, Zeph. Let's check Dad's office." He grabbed his notebook—just in case—and hurried downstairs.

Adam crept inside Dad's office. He wasn't supposed to bother Dad when he was working, but this was an emergency. "Hey, Dad," he said, peeking in.

"Hey, Adam. What's going on?"

"I thought Mom was taking me to the fire department, but I guess you're supposed to be. Or maybe not. But Mom isn't back yet."

Dad checked his watch? "Oh, I must have gotten confused. Was it written on the calendar? If so, your mom must have forgotten to remind me." He smiled. "That's okay. I was wrapping up anyway. Tonight's the night of your photo shoot, isn't it? You and Zeph."

Adam nodded.

"That's my boy. I can't wait. Not to mention I get to eat crab legs for dinner."

Dad followed Adam out the door, locked his office, and got into the car. Adam smiled. He was going to be on time after all.

~ * ~

At 4:30, Cassie pulled into the Hollingers' driveway. "All ready?" Cassie asked when Courtney ran out.

Courtney nodded. "I got Zeph's wheel cart ready to go. Let me go grab Zeph."

She left the cart in the trunk and went into the house.

"Zeph?"

No one answered.

"Zeph?"

Courtney ran into the family room. Only Sapphie greeted her. She was lounging in Zeph's bed, chewing on a bone.

Courtney's ears pounded. She just remembered: Adam had taken Zeph to the fire hall tonight. It was the night of the big photo shoot. Everyone had gotten confused, and Zeph was needed in two places at once. "And Sapphie is needed nowhere," she mumbled.

Courtney hurried outside. Sapphie followed. "Cassie,

176

we have a problem."

Cassie kept her face calm. "Take a deep breath, and then tell me what's wrong."

"Zeph is gone. He's with Adam. He had to be at an event at the fire hall."

"Oh no." Cassie took a few deep breaths. "If we call the fire hall and explain, I'm sure Adam will understand. They can reschedule, right? I mean, a play is more important than—"

Courtney shook her head. "I think tonight means a lot to Adam. If I call him, he's going to blame me for messing things up again. I literally just talked to him, and I didn't say anything about Zeph." Courtney sighed. "The thing is, I wrote it down correctly on the calendar. Adam's the one who got the dates wrong. That's three times he's messed up lately. I can't wait to have a word with him. Three strikes and you're out!"

Cassie held up her hand. "There will be time for that later. For now, we have to figure out what to do about the play."

Both of them turned to Sapphie. She sat, staring up at them, and yelped. Her entire body wagged.

"Do you think she can handle it?" Cassie asked.

Courtney looked at Sapphie. "Can you be good?"

"Rooo!" Sapphie cried.

"Does that sound like a 'yes' to you, Cassie?"

"It'll have to. Grab her leash and let's go. We still have time for a bit of a dress rehearsal. We can modify her part if she won't cooperate. But I have to make a quick stop back at my house. There's something I need."

In the car on the way to Red Rose Middle School, Courtney reviewed all the commands she'd taught Sapphie at obedience school. "She knows 'speak,' or at least she's supposed to, so I can tell her to speak when she's supposed to howl at the characters. She also knows 'quiet.' She doesn't know 'chase,' but maybe if we have the characters she's supposed to chase whisper 'here, Sapphie,' she'll chase them."

Cassie nodded but kept her eyes on the road. "I've seen a big improvement in Sapphie. I think she can do it. Together—with you—she can do this."

~ Twenty-Three ~

There was already a line at the door by the time Adam arrived.

"Wow, the crab leg feed really is the most popular event." Adam looked down at Zeph. "Hope you're ready to meet lots of people."

Dad scratched his head. "I guess I should wait in line, then, to make sure I get a seat."

"I guess so. I'll see you inside."

Dad smiled. "I wouldn't miss the chance for a picture with Zeph!"

"Arooo!" Zeph howled.

Adam laughed and pulled him toward the volunteer entrance. Inside, Spencer was standing by the kitchen window, as usual. Spencer smirked as Adam approached.

"Here's the hero of the day."

Adam detected a hint of bitterness in his voice.

"Hi, Spencer. This is my dog, Zeph."

"So this is the dog everyone's been talking about."

Adam nodded. Spencer bent down to pet Zeph, but Zeph skittered behind Adam.

Adam laughed nervously. "He must be freaked out by all the people here."

Spencer rolled his eyes. "He'd better un-freak out soon. The number of people is going to increase."

"Okay," Adam said. "So what do you want me to do?"

Spencer shook his head. "Nothing tonight. Chief Kurle says you're to sit at the raffle table the whole night. Spark's going to announce the event. She's got a whole speech prepared about you and your dog. She's been rehearsing it in the garage since she got here." He rolled his eyes again. "So hop to it. Go sit on your throne. All the rest of us volunteers will have to pick up your slack. I'll be selling fifty-fifty raffle tickets again with Bill, so I guess Emily and Gavin will have to pick up the slack you're leaving behind. Hope you're happy, hero."

"Good grief," Adam mumbled as he walked toward the raffle table. He sat down and set his notebook on the table. He turned to Zeph. "We've got to be extra observant tonight. There could be some fishy stuff going on. Riley Couth would say to keep a sharp eye. Can you do that, boy?"

Zeph wagged his tail. "Whoo!"

"Good boy."

Adam looked over his list of suspects. Bill. Spencer. Emily. Gavin. Of course, it could be someone unknown. Maybe someone with connections. Riley Couth would start by eliminating suspects. Adam underlined Emily's name. Surely it couldn't be her.

He looked up, and sure enough, Emily was standing at the other end of the fire hall. He waved at her, and she walked over.

"Adam! Congratulations on this photo shoot. Are you excited?"

"A little nervous, I guess."

Emily smiled, and she spun her head around the room. Then she turned back to Adam. "I'm worried about tonight. We were only ten dollars short last time, but we were keeping track using the popcorn bags. Tonight's main source of income—besides your photos—is the fifty-fifty raffle. We're going to have to keep track of the number of tickets sold. But we usually sell around five hundred of those. There's no way to keep track of them all until after the raffle—when someone has to sit down and count all the non-winning tickets."

Adam scratched his head.

"Keep an eye on the money jar."

"Are you saying that Spencer—"

Emily shook her head. "I'm not sure who it is, but I'm sure if they're going to steal anything tonight, it's going to disappear from that money jar. I hear you're a detective of sorts." Emily smiled.

Adam nodded. "I'll keep my eyes open." When she left, Adam looked at his notebook again. He wanted to cross off Emily's name, but Courtney's voice echoed in his mind, so he left it alone.

Before long, Spark arrived. She was as energetic as ever, and she carried a large banner. "Hey, Hollinger, help me hang this up." She handed him a roll of tape.

"What's this for?"

"I thought we could have the Stoney Brook Fire Company logo as the backdrop to your pictures. What do you think?"

"Looks good." Adam smiled.

"What's wrong? You nervous?"

"No."

"Your dog nervous?"

"No."

"Then smile a little. No one will want a picture of someone who isn't smiling."

Adam forced a smile.

"You sure nothing's wrong?"

Adam nodded.

"Okay, then. I'm going to go practice one more time for your grand introduction. Then I'll be back."

Adam waited for Spark to leave before he scribbled her name at the bottom of the list of suspects. He doubted it was her, but he couldn't eliminate anyone at this point. Just as he did so, a shadow blocked the light. Adam looked up.

"Fire Chief Kurle!" Adam smiled.

"Adam! Good to see you." He pulled up a chair. "I decided I'm going to collect the money for the photos tonight." He laughed. "I'll also be taking the pictures. But on a serious note, I want to keep an eye on the cash. It seems the money around here has a tendency to grow legs and walk away. And money that walks away is money that can't be used for equipment, and equipment saves lives."

Adam nodded.

Kurle leaned in close. "You haven't seen or heard anything fishy, have you?"

Adam shook his head.

"Well, you let me know, okay? I'll be back in a few minutes."

Adam frowned and added Fire Chief Kurle's name to the list. At this point, no one could be eliminated.

Another shadow blocked the light, and a loud *clank* jarred Adam from his notes. "Here you go," Spencer said, pushing a glass jar toward Adam. "It's like the one I carry around with Bill. Chief Kurle told me to give it to you. You know, to collect money for photos."

"Thanks," Adam said.

Spencer narrowed his eyes. "Make sure all the money in that jar *stays* in that jar." He furrowed his brow and walked away without another word. On the other side of the room, he nodded to Emily, who opened the door in the coat room. With the loud din of chatter, a crowd started trickling in to the fire hall. Adam already felt his ears burning at the possible attention he might receive. He looked down at Zeph and scratched him behind the ears.

"It's going to be a long night, boy."

~ * ~

Mr. Marty and Miss Gloria had already arrived by the time Courtney and Cassie brought Sapphie into the auditorium.

"Why, hello, Zeph, our little star!" Miss Gloria sang, running up to pet Zeph.

Sapphie wagged her tail.

"He seems happy to be here," she said, bending to pet Sapphie.

"Um..." Courtney cleared her throat.

"It isn't Zeph," said Cassie.

"Huh?"

"Zeph wasn't home. This is his sister, Sapphie. She's going to have to play the role tonight."

182

Miss Gloria's face blanched. "You mean this is the Sapphie that—c-c-caused a ruckus during auditions?"

Courtney gulped. "Yes."

"And how do we know she won't cause a ruckus tonight?"

"We don't," Courtney mumbled.

Cassie snapped her fingers. "Yes, we do. Courtney has been taking Sapphie to obedience classes, and I have personally seen an improvement in Sapphie." She winked at Courtney and said, much more quietly, "Besides, I have a little trick up my sleeve."

Miss Gloria crossed her arms. "I don't see how this little puppy is going to not only behave herself, but do tricks on all her cues. She's never been to a rehearsal."

"Watch this," said Cassie. She held up her hand. She wore a long purple shirt with wide, flowing sleeves. Embellished with rhinestones, they caught the lighting of the auditorium and sparkled in the air. "Sapphie, come." Sapphie immediately snapped up, walked away from Miss Gloria, and sat calmly at Cassie's feet.

Miss Gloria frowned. "Okay, Cassie. I'm trusting you on this one. But I still don't like it."

"Zeph will be here tomorrow," Courtney muttered. But Miss Gloria had already turned toward the dressing rooms backstage.

"Cassie," Courtney whispered. "How did you do that? Maybe you *are* magic!"

"I told you." She winked again. "I have a trick up my sleeve." She rolled up her wide sleeve, revealing a piece of comforter that looked very familiar. Courtney looked back at Sapphie, who still sat intently. Her nose twitched from time to time.

Cassie laughed. "Remember that comforter Arabella and I brought out the day you found the kittens? They've been sleeping on it ever since."

"I know. Before you and Belle agreed to keep the kittens at your house, Sapphie wouldn't leave their side."

Cassie nodded. "Yep. Which is why I cut off a little scrap of the comforter. It must smell like Shadow and the kittens." She snapped her fingers. Sapphie sat at attention. "Hopefully, the scent will keep her focused and calm for the evening. Roll up your sleeve. I'm going to stick a scrap in your sleeve, too, so that Sapphie will have to listen to you. I'm also going to give one to Bobby, who plays Mister Baxter. He's always on stage, so that way, Sapphie will have one more character that smells like her cats."

Courtney smiled widely. "I never would have thought of this." Cassie handed her a scrap, which she put in her sleeve. "Sapphie, come." She took two steps back, and Sapphie followed, her nose twitching in the air. Courtney squealed in delight. "I don't know how to thank you, Cassie."

"Thank me after the show. For now, we've got to get Sapphie strapped into the cart and teach her how to walk in it. Remember, we didn't even get that far during auditions!"

Courtney nodded and pointed to the cart. She held up her arm—the one hiding the scrap of comforter. "Sapphie, come."

Sapphie walked calmly to the cart and started to climb in. Courtney looked over to see if Cassie noticed, but Cassie was marking some things on a script. Courtney turned back to her dog in wonder. Maybe Sapphie *was* a genius. She acted as if she already knew how the cart worked—and she'd never seen it in action before!

For the first time since she arrived, Courtney took a deep breath. Maybe opening night wouldn't be such a disaster after all.

~ Twenty-Four ~

Food wasn't served at the crab feed until six o'clock—even though crowds started filing in at five. The smell of seafood in the air—delicious snow crab legs, cream of crab soup, and fries—was driving everyone crazy with hunger. Spark came up to Adam's table, where the microphone was hooked up, and took every advantage of the situation.

"Goooood evening, folks! Welcome to the SBFC. Dinner will be served shortly, but in the meantime, we've got several ways for you to have some fun and benefit your friendly, local fire company while you're doing it." Adam watched her hold the microphone in one hand and motion around the room with the other. She looked and sounded so natural. She must have been born with such confidence.

"Our first opportunity is back there near the kitchen window." She pointed to Spencer and Bill. "Spencer, Bill, wave to everyone!" The two boys waved. "These two gentlemen will be coming around selling fifty-fifty raffle tickets. The winner of the raffle will go home with half of all the money earned for tickets sold. The crab leg dinner is always a sold-out event, so the fifty-fifty raffle should be high tonight—usually averaging over five hundred dollars!"

The room filled with awed chatter.

"But remember, folks, you can't win if you don't play, so buy your tickets now, before your hands get all messy from the crab legs!" She turned to Adam. "We have an extra special opportunity tonight—a photo opp, to be exact! You may have heard about Stoney Brook's own fifth-grade hero. Last summer, he tracked down a serial burglar in his own neighborhood. This burglar had stumped the cops, folks. We're talking a fifth-grade detective. That's right, our very own Adam Hollinger is here to pose in pictures with his heroic dog, Zeph."

Adam waved to the crowd. He could tell his ears and face were as red as his baseball cap and t-shirt. He hoped he cooled down before people started taking pictures.

"Adam is also a star pitcher for the Autumn League and narrowly lost the Autumn League championships to the harrowing Altoona Angels. Not to mention his near-famous corgi, Zeph. Zeph is the smartest corgi you'll ever meet, folks. He's awesome, and he howls like this." She placed the microphone in front of Zeph and whispered "speak."

Zeph howled into the microphone, a loud "Aroooooo!" filling the fire hall.

The crowd cheered and clapped. A few even stood up to start to get in line.

"For a suggested donation of only five dollars, you can get your picture taken with Zeph and Adam, or just Zeph, if you prefer. Your pictures will be taken by our own photographer, Fire Chief Kurle, who will email you a high resolution digital copy tonight."

Adam looked at Spark and raised his eyebrow. He couldn't see any notecards or anything like that. Spark was speaking from memory. He didn't know how she did it. If it were up to Adam to give a speech like that, he wouldn't be able to get out the first three words.

Adam looked around the room. All over, people were getting up, looking in their wallets for money, and making their way over to his table. He searched the room for Gavin—he was in the corner putting a huge black trash bag in one of the cans and didn't see Adam. He always looked so diligent. It was difficult to believe Gavin would ever choose to steal money from a fire company. After all, if Gavin needed money, it would be easier for him to think of an entrepreneurial idea. Gavin was smart that way. Maybe Courtney was right. After all, sometimes even Riley Couth had to trust his gut.

Adam bent down to his notebook again and crossed through Gavin's name. Gavin was no longer a suspect. Petting Zeph, Adam swept the rest of the room the way

Riley Couth always did. Most of the people looked hungry or relaxed. Fire Chief Kurle was coming this way, playing with the settings of an expensive-looking camera, but even he looked relatively relaxed. In the opposite corner, near another of the trash cans, Emily and Bill were talking. They were lining the trash can with a black plastic bag, but it seemed to be taking them forever. They were leaning together as if they were trying to keep their voices low.

Adam raised an eyebrow. Could Courtney have been right about Emily? He shook his head. She was probably asking Bill questions to see if he was a suspect. That was probably it. He picked up his pencil to cross through her name, too, but Fire Chief Kurle arrived before he could do so.

"Look at this line!" he said, patting Adam on the back. "All these people want pictures with you and Zeph!"

Indeed, a line had formed at the table. Kurle set the jar at the edge of the table. "Alright, now Adam, you set Zeph up on the table, and you stand behind him." He backed up with his camera to make sure the shot was just right. "No, no...scoot over a little. To your right. No, your other right."

Finally, Adam was standing in the perfect position. Zeph sat on the table, looking curiously back at Adam. "Good boy," Adam whispered. "Sit. Stay."

"Okay!" Fire Chief Kurle said, setting up a tripod to hold the camera. "Anyone who wants a picture with Zeph and Adam, write down your email address on the sheet of paper next to the donation jar. Then drop in your donation. Write neatly so I'll know where to send your pictures. Write neatly!"

The first person to arrive was a rambunctious little girl. She wore a pink dress and two pigtails. "Just the doggie!" she said. Her father scribbled his email address on the paper and then lifted her up so she could drop a five-dollar bill into the donations jar. He looked apologetically at Adam.

"Zeph, stay," Adam said as he backed away.

The father placed the girl on the table next to Zeph. She threw her arms around him.

"Whoo?" Zeph howled as the fire chief snapped the picture.

"Nice doggie!" she squealed.

"Let's get one more," Kurle said. "I think her eyes were closed."

"Thanks, kid," the girl's father told Adam. Then he lifted his daughter and brought her back to his table. Adam could still hear her singing, "Nice doggie!" from the other side of the room.

The next person in line was a hurried-looking woman who wore purple reading glasses hanging from a string around her neck. She reached out a hand to Adam. It was ice cold. "Glad to meet you. I'm Geraldine Parks. I teach over at Cold Spring Middle School. I taught Bianca last year. She's told our class about you, and when I heard you'd be here, I thought I should stop by and get my picture taken with a local hero."

Adam felt himself blushing.

"And I heard you and Zeph helped a local student do some research for her doctoral degree?"

"Yes," Adam sighed. "That was my neighbor, Belle. She was doing some research over the summer."

Mrs. Parks posed for the camera. Once the flash went off, she shook Adam's hand again. "I love meeting young people who I know will grow up to do great things. Then I can say, 'I knew him when...'."

The line of people continued. Most of the kids wanted to take pictures only with Zeph. The grown-ups took pictures with Adam, too. By the time Adam had a chance to look at the glass jar, it was getting pretty full.

Adam looked at the next person in line. It was a face he recognized: Gavin.

"Gavin?" Adam laughed. "You know you can get a picture of me anytime you want. We're friends."

Gavin's eyes lit up. "It's just that I don't have a

picture of us together, so I thought..." He dropped five dollars into the jar. "I made a lot of money in tips over Thanksgiving." He smiled.

Another person to step up looked familiar, but Adam couldn't place the face.

"I'm a local coach," the man said. "I won't remind you what team I coach." He laughed. "But you beat us pretty good as a member of the Lancaster Reds. Anyway, even though we don't play for the same team, I recognize talent when I see it, and I'd love to get a picture with the star pitcher."

Adam smiled. "Thanks."

Eventually, Adam recognized another face: Emily.

"You, too, Emily? You know you can get a picture with me anytime you want, too."

She nodded. "I know. But I like to do my part for the fire company." She dropped a five-dollar bill into the jar. Then she looked at the fire chief.

"This jar is getting pretty full, Kurle. Want me to organize it for you?"

"Good idea, Emily," he said from behind the camera. "Why don't you do that after you've had your picture taken?"

She posed for a photo with Adam and Zeph, and then she stepped to the side and grabbed a handful of five-dollar bills, smoothing them out.

"Excuse me, miss," one of the guests said. "Can you give me change for a twenty?"

"Sure." Adam watched as Emily counted out three five-dollar bills for him.

"Thanks."

"Me, too," another guest requested. "I only have a twenty-dollar bill. Just came from the ATM."

"Emily," Fire Chief Kurle said. "You stay here until they serve dinner. Make change for guests, and keep that money jar under control and under close watch."

"Sure thing, Chief!"

The next guest in line was very familiar. Adam rolled his eyes and smiled. "Da-ad! You can get a picture of me anytime you want."

"Yes, but when can I get a picture of you, Zeph, and the Stoney Brook Fire Company banner in the background *and* help out the fire company while I'm at it?"

Dad dropped five one-dollar bills into the jar. Emily promptly snatched them out and smoothed them, adding them to her stack.

"Thanks, Dad." Adam posed with his father.

The evening stretched on. As it got closer to six o'clock, the line dwindled. People returned to their tables, hoping they would be the first number called to eat. At one minute to six, Spark got back on the microphone. "Alright, folks. We'll start calling table numbers now. When your table is called, go ahead to the buffet table. Give your ticket to Gavin. Gavin, give everyone a wave! We'll still be taking pictures here in this corner, so if you haven't gotten to take a picture yet with these two young heroes, you still have time. Alright, the first table to get in line for food is..."

Adam turned to Emily to ask how much money they had made so far, but when he looked up, his mouth went dry. There was Marnie Ellison, dressed in red pants and a black sweater with sparkly red clips in her hair.

"Hi, Adam. I thought I'd get a picture with the local hero and his dog." Marnie smiled and nudged Adam toward Zeph and stood facing the camera. She put her arm around his shoulders. Adam tried to remember to breathe, and he wondered how red his ears would look in the picture.

"Say cheese!" Chief Kurle said.

"Cheese!" Marnie repeated.

"Whoo!" said Zeph.

"Are you here for the crab feed?" Adam asked.

Marnie nodded and pointed. "There's my mom and dad. My sister's here, too. She was hoping Courtney would be here."

Adam shook his head. "No, Courtney's got her play

tonight."

"A play?"

"Yep, she's in this play, and Zeph is actually—" Adam swallowed a lump in his throat.

"What's wrong, Adam?"

"I—I think I may have ruined Courtney's evening."

"What is it? I'll just have my sister text her."

"Courtney won't be checking her phone if she's at the school. I just hope she doesn't get too mad at me."

Adam craned his neck, looking for his dad, but the crowd overwhelmed the room, and Adam couldn't tell the difference between one person and the next. Everything blurred together.

"You look upset." Marnie smiled sadly. "I'll leave you to your pictures." She pointed to the last few people who stood in line. "Take it easy, Adam. I'm sure Courtney's fine. I'll see you at school on Monday."

She smiled, but Adam was too disturbed to smile back. How could he have forgotten that Courtney was borrowing Zeph for her play—on the same night Adam needed Zeph for the pictures? And why hadn't Mom or Courtney contacted Dad about it?

Adam breathed a sigh of relief when the line ended. Everyone was eager to eat, and Adam was eager for a break. Fire Chief Kurle sat down behind the table and turned to Emily, who was sitting behind the jar. It now contained a neat stack of money, all rolled up inside.

"Nice job, Emily. Why don't you go help Gavin with the tickets, and then check the trash bags to make sure they're not too full? Take Gavin with you."

Emily frowned. "Can I take Bill with me instead?"

Kurle rubbed his moustache. "I don't see why not, but what's wrong with Gavin?"

"He's just little is all." Emily smiled. "It's hard for him to reach the dumpster."

Kurle shrugged. "Suits me. Take Bill with you to bring the trash out to the dumpster, then. The trash cans fill up fast during crab feeds—everyone throwing away crab shells and dozens and dozens of napkins!"

Spark continued calling tables to get in line for crabs while Kurle counted the money.

"How many names are on that email list, Adam?" he asked.

Adam counted. "Forty-seven."

"You sure?"

Adam nodded.

Kurle finished counting for a second time. "I'm coming up with $205."

"It should be..." Adam rubbed his chin. "$235."

"You're good at math, too." Kurle smiled. "What aren't you good at?" He cleared his throat. "But sadly, this means that thirty dollars somehow walked away. Only three people were near that money. Me, you, and Emily."

"I didn't take any of it." Adam's ears burned.

"I didn't say you did, son. I've been watching you the whole time from the other side of the camera. You wouldn't have had time to take any of that money even if you wanted to. And I sure as heck didn't take money from my own fire company. That would be like stealing money to endanger my own life. We need that upgraded equipment. That leaves..."

"Maybe it wasn't Emily." Adam swallowed a lump in his throat. "Maybe one of the people in line took it. Or maybe Emily messed up when making change."

The fire chief's face softened. "Maybe you're right. Maybe she did get mixed up." He smiled. "You're right, Adam. Emily wouldn't steal from us." He patted Adam on the back. "Why don't you go get some food?"

Spark cheered into the microphone. "The last table to get in line for food—finally—is table number one! Take all you like, but eat all you take."

The room erupted in cheers and then promptly silenced as everyone focused on eating.

~ Twenty-Five ~

Zeph's nose twitched. There were an awful lot of people, and all of them coming up to him, too. And so many pictures. Zeph wasn't quite sure what was happening. But he kept hearing people say "fire hall" and "fire company," so he knew he was close to the location of extra fire.

Even though Shadow was safe now, it was still a good idea to see where fire came from. Maybe he could even sneak some fire back home with him. Sapphie would be interested in it, and maybe Shadow would want to play with it, too. Perhaps Sapphie could help bury some fire in the backyard in case they needed it later on—in case the days kept getting colder.

But where did this fire company keep its fire?

Zeph's nose twitched again. There were so many smells coming from the kitchen. This company obviously had a lot of fire in order to make all that food. Perhaps the fire came from the kitchen.

A person who looked similar to Mom was talking to Adam, and Zeph cocked his head to listen.

"I think it's great you're doing this for the fire company. It's great to involve volunteers at such a young age. You know, I remember a few years ago when they had a fundraiser to purchase that fire truck out in the garage. It's saved countless lives by now. I don't know how much that fire truck actually cost, but it's priceless, isn't it? I mean, you can't put a price on a human life."

Adam reached out and shifted Zeph over on the table. The woman who looked like Mom put a hand on his head, and the camera snapped.

Zeph cocked his head after she left. So there was a fire truck in the garage out back. A fire truck was probably used to deliver fire. If Zeph could only sneak out into the

193

garage, maybe he could snatch a little piece of fire. But he wasn't good at sneaking. If only Sapphie were here. She would find a way.

But she wasn't here. So Zeph tucked back his ears and watched Adam, listening for any opportunity that might take him into the garage where the Stoney Brook Fire Company kept all of the extra fire it made.

~ * ~

Sapphie surprised everyone during the dress rehearsal, and Courtney, in full costume, stood in front of the mirror with confidence. She leaned on her prop crutches and fixed her baseball cap, which she wore backwards. She cleared her throat and practiced her first line, which was the second line in the entire play.

"I'm looking for a book." Then the owner of the store was supposed to ask her what kind of book. Then Courtney was supposed to say, "I need a good book that will take a long time to read."

She cleared her throat and tried again, accenting different syllables this time. "I need a good book that will take a *long* time to read. Time to *read*. *Time* to read."

Cassie peeked into the dressing room.

"All ready, Courtney?"

Courtney looked down at Sapphie, who sat patiently in her cart.

"All set."

Cassie smiled. "I'm so impressed with Sapphie. She drives that cart like a professional, and I swear she knows which characters she's supposed to bark at, which she's supposed to howl at, and which she's supposed to chase. I'm beginning to wonder if we even need the scraps of kitty comforter."

Courtney laughed. "I wouldn't test it."

"Neither would I." She took a deep breath. "I'm going to go out and introduce myself, and then we'll get started."

Courtney took a sip of water from the bottle that

had been left back stage and labeled with her name. Her name was written in purple—her favorite color—and decorated with gold and silver star stickers. She couldn't help but smile. Then she knelt down and pet Sapphie. "If you ever were good in your life, Sapphie, please be good tonight."

Sapphie licked her lips and cocked her head. Applause filled the auditorium. They were clapping for Cassie. Courtney heard her start to speak and knew she had only a moment before her entrance.

"Be good," she whispered one more time.

"Curtain!" Miss Gloria shouted.

Courtney propped herself up on her crutches and headed toward the stage. "Sapphie," she whispered. "Come."

Sapphie pulled herself in the cart, following right behind Courtney. As they entered the stage, the auditorium was dark, and the lights were blinding. But as soon as Sapphie wheeled herself onto the stage, the darkened auditorium filled with "awww's" and "how cute's." The praise seemed to build Sapphie's ego. She puffed out her chest and sped her pace, racing around the stage in wide circles as if to show off her skills.

Courtney hobbled toward the bookstore, which was a separate platform on stage. Sapphie didn't follow. "Denby, come on," she improvised.

"Sapphie," she whispered. She held up her arm—the one with the cat comforter—and Sapphie made her way over.

Bobby cleared his throat. "Welcome to Mister Baxter's Books. I'm Mister Baxter. How can I help you?"

Courtney smiled and peeked into the audience. She couldn't see Mom, but she knew she was there. Then she turned back to Bobby. "I'm looking for a book."

Bobby held up his hands. "What kind of book?"

Courtney leaned on her crutch. "I need a good book that will take a long time to read." She looked down at her dog. "My name's Dani, and this is my dog, Denby. We've been recently injured in a—"

Right on cue, Melinda entered, dressed as a bratty little girl looking for a candy store. Sapphie howled at her right away, like she was supposed to. Courtney looked at Bobby. Bobby shrugged. Neither of them had even given Sapphie her cue. Courtney took a deep breath as Melinda spoke her lines.

This play was going really well after all.

~ * ~

Adam walked Zeph into the room behind the kitchen, where Spark was sitting eating a huge bowl of soup.

"You don't want any crabs?" he asked.

Spark shook her head. "This is the best soup I've had in my entire life. Bill's dad makes it, and it's got plenty of crab in it. Here, I got you a bowl." She pointed to a smaller bowl on the table.

"Thanks."

"You looked busy over there. The soup always runs out at the end of these dinners, and I wanted to make sure you got some."

"That was nice of you."

Spark smiled. "I try. Besides, a friend of Courtney is a friend of mine."

Adam smiled. He reached into his pocket. "I almost forgot, Zeph. Here are some treats I brought for you." He placed several bacon strips and a few biscuits on the floor.

"Arooo!" Zeph howled.

Adam knew he wasn't supposed to tell anyone about the missing money, but he felt he could trust Spark. He leaned in close. "Do you know there's been money walking away from this place?"

Spark shrugged. "Wasn't me."

"I wasn't saying it was. I was wondering if you knew who it might be."

"I'd guess Spencer in an instant."

"Really? Why?" Adam had left his notebook at the photo table, but he mentally went through the list of remaining suspects.

"Have you ever talked to him? What's not to suspect? He loves being in charge way too much, and he kept bothering Chief Kurle to be left in charge of volunteers and be allowed to handle money. It all seems suspicious."

"But why would he take the money?"

Spark shrugged.

"What do you know about Bill?"

"Not too much. His dad was a firefighter, but he got injured. Bill's been bitter ever since. The family's always short on money, and word is that Bill's going to quit volunteering here as soon as he's old enough to get a job. His family doesn't want him to quit, though. His dad still loves this place, even after his injury."

"Hmmm."

"He might want the money, but I doubt he'd take it with his dad right there. If he did, and he was caught, it would be a major embarrassment to his family."

"And what about Emily?"

Spark raised an eyebrow. "You think Emily would do such a thing? She's so helpful and friendly. I highly doubt it."

Adam peeked into the kitchen. Spencer was visible standing outside the kitchen, at the window. He looked like he was counting and marking things on his clipboard again. Adam took a sip of soup to give himself time to think.

"Wow, this is delicious!"

"I told you." Spark smiled. "I come for the soup."

Adam ate the rest of the soup in silence while thinking about the list of suspects. He tried to picture Riley Couth solving this crime, and he couldn't help thinking that he knew where to look.

It even seemed like Zeph knew where to look, too. The dog kept barking and howling and pulling toward the back exit, the one leading to the huge garage.

"Excuse me, Spark. I need to take Zeph outside."

Zeph barked urgently.

"Okay. Have fun. I'm going to keep eating this soup." She smiled and went back to slurping.

Adam peeked into the fire hall. He noticed that all the trash cans were now empty, and Emily and Bill were gone. Zeph kept whining and pulling Adam toward the back exit, and Adam nodded. He knelt down. "We're going outside," he told Zeph. "But you've got to be quiet. We're on a secret mission."

"Hollinger!" a voice called from across the room.

Adam turned to see Spencer running toward him with a clipboard.

"What's wrong?"

Spencer looked upset and was out of breath when he spoke. "While everyone was eating, I decided to double-check the amount of money in our jar with the number of tickets sold."

"That must have taken forever."

"The tickets are all numbered. I kept track of which ticket number we started with. It wasn't that difficult. Anyway, we're fifty-seven dollars short."

"Fifty-seven," Adam whispered. "Plus thirty. That's a total of eighty-seven dollars missing tonight." He turned to Spencer. "Thirty dollars disappeared from the picture jar."

"Did you see anything?"

Adam bit his lip. "I didn't see anything, but I think I know what's going on. I was just about to go check."

Spencer narrowed his eyes. "I'm coming with you." He motioned across the room, where Fire Chief Kurle was eating. Kurle stood up and hurried toward the boys.

"Adam thinks he knows who's been stealing the money," Spencer told the fire chief. "Let's follow him."

Adam snuck out the back door and headed toward the dumpster. Zeph pulled toward the garage, but Adam shortened his leash, keeping him close. "Hush," he reminded the dog. In the evening darkness, he could make out only the shiny bulge of four plastic trash bags. "There," he whispered. He snuck closer, with Spencer and Kurle following close behind.

They ducked behind a car and listened.

"Ten, fifteen, twenty, twenty-five, thirty." One figure handed a stack of bills to another.

"And here—they're all singles. Give me a minute to count. One, two, three..."

"It's Bill," Spencer whispered.

"And Emily," said Kurle.

"That makes fifty-seven," Bill said.

"That's eighty-seven. Not exactly enough for a washer, but added to what we got the last few weeks, that makes—"

"We're up to two-hundred twelve dollars. I think that's good enough to get one at a second-hand store. It will be a great Christmas surprise for Mom. Thanks for helping me, Emily."

"Hey, what are friends for?" The two figures embraced. Adam's heart sank.

Fire Chief Kurle growled. Then he sighed. He stepped out of the shadows, turning on the flashlight he always kept on his belt. "Everyone stop right there."

The two figures started to dart away.

"Emily, Bill, I already know it's you. No use running away. Come over here."

The two approached. Emily was already in tears.

"It's not what it looks like." She sniffled.

Behind him, Adam heard Spencer dash inside.

"Really?" The fire chief put a hand on his hip and shined the flashlight at Emily and Bill. "Because what it looks like to me is two of my volunteers have been skimming money from my fundraisers."

"I can explain." Bill choked on his words.

"His family's washing machine broke."

"We've fixed it several times. We can't afford a new

one right now, and Mom's devastated."

"So you thought you'd steal from a fire company?"

Zeph plopped to the ground and whined.

"Well, what have you got to say for yourself?"

"I—" Bill swallowed a sob.

"Bill, you more than anyone should understand the importance of buying updated equipment for our volunteers. Even though he was injured, your father's life was saved because he was wearing new safety equipment during that fire."

"Lot of good it did him," Bill spat.

"It *did* do him good. Your father's alive. There's a lot of people who can't say the same. By stealing from the fire company, you may be depriving another child of a father. What about Spark? Don't you want her father to be protected?"

Adam turned toward a set of footsteps approaching. Spencer was back. Behind him, limping with a cane, was a man who Adam guessed to be Bill's father, the man injured in a fire.

The fire chief turned to him. "William..."

Mr. Blazier turned to his son. "Bill, is it true? Is it true what Spencer told me? Have you been stealing from the fire company?"

Bill broke down in tears. "It's not what you think. I was trying to get money to buy Mom a new washing machine."

In the light of Kurle's flashlight, Adam could see a tear fall from Mr. Blazier's eye. Kurle turned the flashlight away and sighed. "I'm not going to press charges, William. We can handle this internally. It seems like somewhat of a misunderstanding."

He turned to Emily and Bill. "Even if your intentions are good, it doesn't make what you did acceptable. What you did is a crime. It's stealing. If I wanted to, I could call the police. The two of you are what, fourteen? Fifteen? You're getting to the age where you could get into serious trouble for committing a crime. We've got a lot of talking to do." He turned to Adam.

"Adam, Spencer. Thanks for your help. I think you two should go back inside now. Adam, have Spark announce a last call for photos and raffle tickets. Here." He snatched the eighty-seven dollars and handed it to Spencer. "Put thirty back in the photo jar. The other goes to the fifty-fifty."

Spencer nodded. Emotional voices rose in the darkness as Adam and Spencer walked inside. Spencer gave Adam's arm a friendly punch. "I was wrong about you, Hollinger. And it turns out Fire Chief Kurle was right. You really do have the blood of a hero. Welcome to Stoney Brook Fire Company."

~ * ~

On stage, Courtney had just two more lines to go. Her heart pounded. The entire play had gone so well. Sapphie knew every cue, and when she wasn't doing anything, she was sitting attentively, staring at Courtney's sleeve.

"I think they all learned a lesson today," Bobby, in the character of Mr. Baxter, said. "And I learned that all lessons don't necessarily come from books."

Courtney shrugged and laughed as she limped toward the door. "Sometimes it's easy to forget what a gift each day is. But it shouldn't take a daredevil, or her courageous pup, to remind everyone to live each day to its fullest."

"And not to let little problems take over."

"That's right," Courtney, as Daring Dani, said. "Now come on, Denby Dog." She patted her leg. "Let's get going—onward and upward. Another adventure awaits. I guess you never know how many lives you can change in any given day."

Sapphie started to follow, but she paused when she reached the center of the stage. Courtney's heart pounded even faster. This was not part of the play, and she wondered what Sapphie was going to do. She'd done so well so far—why would she ruin it now?

Sapphie took one look at the audience and let out a loud "Roooo!" Then she did a series of spins in her cart. The audience went wild, cheering and applauding. Courtney shook her head and smiled. She could swear Sapphie knew exactly what she was doing—and was showing off for the audience. Maybe Sapphie had a talent for improv as well as acting.

Courtney improvised, too, joining Sapphie at center stage and taking a bow. She then pointed behind her to Bobby, who came forward and joined them. Soon, the entire cast was lined up at the edge of the stage, Courtney and Sapphie in the middle, taking bow after bow after bow to a cheering crowd and a standing ovation. Sapphie inched closer to Courtney and, even strapped into the cart, rubbed against her leg the way a cat might—just like Shadow.

~ Twenty-Six ~

The Hollingers crammed into two cars to get to the matinee. Mom drove Adam, Patrick, and Gavin in Dad's sedan. Dad took Courtney to Willow Lakes in Mom's minivan, where they picked up Mr. and Mrs. Grindle, who sat in the middle seats. Mrs. Grindle's wheelchair fit in the back. Mr. Grindle wore his finest clothes, including a bright red bowtie. His wife wore a red dress and pearls. They smiled during the entire car ride.

"It's been years since I've seen a play," Mr. Grindle said. "Isn't that right, Eleanor?"

His wife laughed. "It's been years since I tried to convince you to see one. You were always more interested in watching sports. What happened?"

"Sports got old. So did I. Plays never do." He laughed. "I was young and silly then. You excited, Courtney?"

Courtney smiled back at them. "I am, but I'm also exhausted. It's been a rough few days. Not to mention getting home late from the play last night. And it went so well that I couldn't fall asleep. I couldn't stop smiling. I can't wait until winter break. I want to be able to sleep in sometime."

"You'll have more time once this play is over, though, won't you?" asked Mrs. Grindle.

Courtney giggled. "I've got a few other ideas up my sleeve. I have a feeling they'll be taking up some time, too."

Mr. Grindle and his wife exchanged smiles.

"I didn't get to tell you about the cats, though."

"What cats?" asked Mr. Grindle.

Courtney explained. "My dog found this cat in the woods. She had a bunch of kittens and was cold and hungry. We took her in, and my mom brought her to the vet. The kittens were healthy, luckily. They just needed some shots."

"Some very expensive shots," Dad muttered.

"Yes, but the vet offered us as much of a discount as he could."

Dad sighed.

"Anyway, the neighbors have been watching the kittens for us—see, Sapphie is obsessed with them. We let her visit each day, but we thought it would be best for the kittens to have their own place for now without a little corgi watching them all the time. We found homes for almost all of them. Mrs. Bowers is taking one. Cassie picked a kitten for herself, and she's keeping Shadow, too."

"Who's Shadow?"

"The mother cat. I'm not sure what her name actually is, but she looked like a 'Shadow' to all of us. Maybe because of her gray coloring. Anyway, that's what we named her. We have two cats left. They're both black and white."

"I'm sure you'll find homes for them soon."

"We'd better. Sapphie's getting pretty attached even with the cats being kept at Cassie's. The vet said it'll be a while until they can leave their mother—February, I think. Mom and Dad said we have enough animals at our place, and they don't think we're ready for a cat, too." Courtney laughed. "Sapphie's over there now, guarding the kittens. Belle, Cassie's roommate, is watching all of them while we're at the play. Since Sapphie got to perform last night, we thought Zeph should be able to perform today. I think both of them are happy with the arrangement."

~ * ~

In the car Mom drove, Adam, Gavin, and Patrick sat in the back seat together. Zeph got to sit up front, buckled in with his harness. He looked happy.

"Adam, I can't believe you caught another bad guy. You totally should be a detective when you grow up," Patrick said.

Adam frowned. "They weren't bad guys. They were just confused. They thought they were doing the right thing. It's not like the burglar this summer."

"Still, you solved the crime."

Adam nodded. "I'd rather not talk about it, though." He still felt guilty. He hadn't yet heard what Bill or Emily's punishment would be. He wondered if they'd be allowed to volunteer at the fire company any longer. He knew they both had plans to quit and get jobs when they turned sixteen, anyway.

Gavin nodded. "It will be a little awkward around the fire company for a while, won't it?"

"Chief Kurle was upset. He wants to help Bill's parents, but not the way Bill wanted to. The winner of the fifty-fifty raffle was Mrs. Parks, a teacher at Cold Spring Middle School. Chief was late in getting the money to her because he wanted to count it again and make sure it was all there. Well, he ended up telling her the story of what happened. You know what she did? She took her winnings— a total of $267—and gave it to the fire chief to give to Bill's family. For a new washer! Can you believe that? She told him that there are many ways people can be heroes, and that she thought tonight it was her turn."

Gavin nodded. "Wow."

"I think that was so nice of her," Mom said from up front.

Gavin laughed. "I probably would have kept the money, though. If she invested it, she could make it all back, plus interest. And then she could buy not just one washer, but—"

Adam laughed. "I know, Gavin. If I grow up to be a detective, you should grow up to go into business. And send me some of your money when you get rich!"

All three laughed. Patrick rubbed his chin. "All this has got me thinking, though. I'm not sure what I want to do when I grow up, but the way my dad's training me, I'll be in great shape by that time. I was thinking maybe I could be a firefighter. I know it's hard work, but I never realized how much they do. I mean, can you imagine the world without firefighters?"

Mom smiled into the rearview mirror. "I think that's a great idea, Patrick. I know all three of you will grow up to do great things."

"Speaking of great things, we still have two kittens left. Remember the two I told you about? Did you get a chance to talk to you parents?"

Gavin smiled. "I did. They said since I did such a good job thinking of the plan for Thanksgiving, they thought I'd be responsible enough to look after a cat. They said I could have one."

"Awesome! Patrick, what about you?"

Patrick cleared his throat, then lifted his hand and took a mock-bow. "After the world's best pleading, I finally convinced my dad to say yes."

"Great! The vet says the kittens will be ready for their new homes around the first of February."

"That seems like so long to wait!"

"It'll be here before you know it," Mom said.

"Mom, can I borrow your phone?"

"Sure."

Adam reached into the cupholder up front. "Here's pictures of the two that are left. They're almost twins. They're both black and white, but their markings are a little different." He showed them the picture he'd taken with his mom's phone. He smiled, thinking that in a few weeks, he'd have his own phone, and he'd be able to take his own pictures.

"They do match." Patrick turned to Gavin. "Which is cool. You know, seeing as we'll be friends for a while now. Even though we go to different schools now, they all feed into the same high school."

Gavin smiled. "Then we should give our cats matching names."

All three thought about it. "I know!" Adam said. "How about Riley and Couth?"

"Riley! I love it!" Gavin high-fived Adam.

"Couth." Patrick smiled. "It has a certain ring to it."

When they got to Red Rose Middle School, Zeph puffed out his chest.

"Look at him." Adam giggled. "It's almost like he knows he's about to be a star."

"What do you mean about to be?" Patrick laughed. "He's already a star."

Mom and Dad pulled their cars right next to each other.

Adam grabbed Zeph's leash and helped him out of the car. Dad opened the door and helped out Mr. Grindle.

Adam opened the trunk and took out the wheeling cart, setting it down in front of Zeph. Adam's father took Mrs. Grindle's wheelchair from the back of the minivan and set it up for her, helping her in. Zeph took one look at her and howled, looking at the wheeling cart.

Mrs. Hollinger laughed. "I think he wants to practice in his cart."

Adam giggled and strapped Zeph into the cart. Zeph pranced over to Mrs. Grindle, who laughed and applauded. Mr. Grindle put a hand on his wife's arm. "Look at that, honey. Zeph is showing off for you! Giving you your own private performance." He turned toward the school building. "Well, we better head toward the auditorium now. You all have to wait for this old man. Maybe we'll get there before the opening curtain!"

"I'll walk with Mister Grindle," Dad said.

"Me, too," said Gavin.

"And me," said Patrick.

Dad nodded. "Courtney, why don't you push Mrs. Grindle's wheelchair in, and Adam, you go in with Zeph. That way, Courtney and Zeph can get ready for the show. Adam, we'll meet you and Mrs. Grindle inside the lobby."

Adam nodded.

Courtney grabbed the handles of Mrs. Grindle's chair. Adam noticed that she quickly checked her pockets, but it seemed she left her cell phone in the car. Strangely, she didn't say anything. She didn't even seem bothered by it. Adam shrugged and looked down at his dog.

"Come on, Denby Dog," he told Zeph. Zeph pranced in his racer, keeping pace with Mrs. Grindle's wheelchair.

Mrs. Grindle applauded, her smile stretched from ear to ear. "Good boy. You've got a big performance ahead of you. You've got people to inspire and feats to accomplish. After all, you've got the heart of a hero!"

~ END ~